D0759854

2007

MOUNTAINS PAINTED WITH TURMERIC

LIL BAHADUR CHETTRI

TRANSLATED FROM THE NEPALI BY MICHAEL J. HUTT

COLUMBIA UNIVERSITY PRESS   NEW YORK

A NOVEL

MOUNTAINS

PAINTED WITH TURMERIC

COLUMBIA UNIVERSITY PRESS
Publishers Since 1893
NEW YORK   CHICHESTER, WEST SUSSEX

Photographs (except on title page spread) by Michael J. Hutt

LIBRARY OF CONGRESS CATALOGING-IN-PUBLICATION DATA
Kshatri, Lila Bahadura, 1933–
    [Basaim. English]
    Mountains painted with turmeric / Lil Bahadur Chettri ;
    translated by Michael J. Hutt.
        cm.
    Novel.
    Translated from Nepali.
    Includes bibliographical references.
    ISBN 978-0-231-14356-1 (cloth : alk. paper)
    1. Kshatri, Lila Bahadura, 1933——Translations into English. I. Hutt, Michael
    (Michael J.) II. Title.
PK2598.K73B313   2008
891.4'953—dc22   2007012236

Columbia University Press books are printed on permanent and durable acid-free paper
This book was printed on paper with recycled content.

Printed in the United States of America
c 10 9 8 7 6 5 4 3 2 1

CONTENTS

Basain is a seventy-page novel written in Nepali by Lil Bahadur Chettri (b. 1932/33), a descendant of emigrants from the hills of Nepal who was born and still lives in the state of Assam in northeast India. *Basain*, Chettri's first novel, was published in 1957–58 (this corresponds to the year 2014 in the Bikram calendrical era commonly employed in Nepal). Chettri is the author of two further novels—*Atripta* (The unfulfilled), published in 1969, and *Brahmaputraka Cheuchau* (On the banks of the Brahmaputra), published in 1986—but these remain less well known than his first, which entered its thirtieth reprint in 2006. A Nepali-language feature film based on the book and directed by Subash Gajurel opened in 2005 and was Nepal's entry for the 2006 Academy Awards in Los Angeles.

The word *basain* is a nominalization of the verb *basnu*, "to stay, reside," so it is often translated as "settlement" or "residence." It can also denote settlement in a place other than one's own village or country: to move somewhere else and set up home there is expressed in Nepali as "shifting *basain*." The central character of *Basain* is a peasant farmer named Dhan Bahadur Basnet (Dhané for short). Dhané's family name shows that he is a Chetri by caste, as is the author of the novel. He lives in his ancestral family home in a village whose name we are not told, with his wife, Maina, his small son, and his younger sister, Jhuma. Dhané is beset with calamities from the very start, and the novel chronicles the way his circumstances and his position in village society conspire against him and eventually force him to leave—probably for India, though this is not stated. The *dukha* (suffering, sorrow) endured by ordinary peasants—the exploitation of the poor by the rich and powerful, the prejudice and social conservatism that punishes a woman who has been raped—is the central theme of the book.

A second theme is the warmth and intimacy of village life, from which Dhané and his family are ultimately excluded. Although Dhané quarrels with various individuals during the story, these are all either the powerful "big men" (*thulo manche*) of the village or members of castes who are traditionally held to be of low status. Through all of this, Dhané's friendships with men of equal or similar status remain firm. It is also significant that the downfall of Dhané's sister Jhuma, a beautiful, affectionate, in-nocent personification of all that the male author considers ideal in a Nepali woman, is brought about by a man who is in a sense an outsider, an other. Throughout the original Nepali text, this man, who is a soldier, is referred to as "Rikute," a name derived from the English word "recruit." The term *lahure*, derived from the name of the city Lahore, is the Nepali word used most commonly to denote a Nepali soldier who serves in a foreign army, but it does not occur in this text. Like the language of Gurkha soldiers portrayed elsewhere in Nepali fiction (see Hutt 1989), the soldier's speech is spattered with Urdu and Hindi vocabulary, which Jhuma does not understand, and at several points he is described as a "foreigner" or "stranger" (*pardeshi*, literally, "person of/from another country").

AUTHORSHIP AND INFLUENCES

In his introduction to the novel, modestly entitled "My Endeavor" (*Mero prayas*), Lil Bahadur Chettri explained why he wrote the book. A translation of this introduction follows, interspersed with insights gleaned from an article Chettri published some thirty-five years later (Chettri 1992):

> As I think about it now, I realize that it was nearly three years ago that a friend was talking about Nepali literature: "Just write one small novel, why don't you?" I remember him saying. With his encouragement, I thought a lot about writing a novel, and I sat at the table with my pen in my hand for two or three nights, right up until the time when the hands of the clock join in a single line; I sat there disconsolately, and I groaned. Where to begin? With what subject? Nothing occurred to me.
>
> Eventually, I more or less gave up. "Who invites pain into an unaching head?" I thought, but then one day at Pandu

Station I caught sight of two young men who had just arrived from the hills. In reply to my first question, "Where are you going?" I got the response "We've come down here to look for some work as woodcutters." They answered the many other questions I asked them in their own manner, too.

The way they spoke, their manners and clothing, and their description of their village all struck me as foreign. If any other educated youth who had been born and raised in an environment outside Nepal, as I was, had been in my place, all these things would have seemed foreign to him, too.

In his 1992 article, Chettri recalled that people from the hills of eastern Nepal used to appear in his home district in Assam every winter and that it became something of a habit for him to quiz them about life in their villages. He had spent some time in a Nepalese hill village as a young boy and had some "dim remembrance" of it, but what he gleaned from his interrogations served as a useful supplement. He also picked up many features of the eastern dialect of Nepali and employed them in *Basain* (to his amusement, *littérateurs* in Kathmandu were later to identify these wrongly as "Assamese usages" [35]).[1]

Back to his introduction:

It occurred to me that although the future of people like us, who have made our homes outside Nepal, is tied to the country in which we dwell, our language, literature, and culture are still Nepali, and everyone's own literature and culture are dear to them. In order to become well acquainted with Nepali culture, it is also necessary to be familiar with the environment of the place that is the very heart of that culture. Otherwise it will always seem foreign when we hear authentic Nepali being spoken or listen to someone telling us about the culture that is played out in the village environment in the hills of Nepal.

I started to write the novel, my main purpose being merely to acquaint my readers with the village environment back in the hills. Every year, Nepalis leave the Nepalese hills and come down to Madhes (the lowlands) and Mugalan (India).[2] Do they leave their homes because they wish to? Perhaps that is true of many of them. But for others it is quite a different matter. I chose the misery and mystery that lie at the root of this as the theme of *Basain*.

The work of writing the novel commenced, but because I was then a student, my quarterly and half-yearly exams kept harassing me. Thus I began the book in 1954 but had to postpone working further on it for about a year. Then I would write a page or two when I felt like it and put it away when I didn't, and 1956 passed in that manner. In April 1957, by some inspiration or other, I completed the remaining sections.

In 1992 Chettri recalled that *Basain* actually began life as a short story entitled *Besi* (a *besi* is an area of cultivable land, usually on the floor of a valley). He was encouraged by his friend Chatra Bahadur Gurung to lengthen it, add a proper frame, and make it into a novel. Chatra Bahadur was also instrumental in getting the story published. Chapter 14 of *Basain* is the beginning of this original story.

Basain might not entertain its readers, because that is not its aim. In it I have simply tried to give a picture of the villages in the hills of Nepal. Life in the hills—the joys and sorrows of the villages and the events that happen there—is the essence of *Basain*.

From a literary point of view, the standard of this novel is not high, because I have based it on reality. The dialogue and some of the words in it are kept just as they are used far to the east of Kathmandu, in the villages of Dhankuta, Taplejung, and Bhojpur districts. No sniff of a literary pen will be found in this novel; instead, it provides the readers with the smell of the ferns and bitter-leaves[3] that grow on the hillsides and in the ravines.

I myself was not well acquainted with the environment in the hills, and so, although I consulted my friends from the hills where appropriate, my writing will probably be less than satisfactory in many places, and I will probably have failed to give a complete picture of a village. Also, because I am an infant who has only just begun to crawl about in the field of literature, many mistakes will have been overlooked, and the style will not be especially interesting. But if readers will remember that this is my first step on the path of the novel and will forgive me for this and offer me the necessary advice, I shall take note of their comments for the future.

Some years later, Chettri was to read Pearl S. Buck's *The Good Earth* and watch Satyajit Ray's film *Pather Panchali*, and in 1992 he wrote that *Basain* would have been improved if these influences had been incorporated. Twelve years after writing *Basain*, he also read Lainsingh Bangdel's important Nepali novel *Muluk Bahira* (Outside the country). Bangdel's novel is concerned with the lives of several characters who have migrated from eastern Nepal to Darjeeling: Chettri writes that it struck him as "the Nepali reality that comes after *Basain*" (1992:36).[4]

About the task of publishing the book, Chettri wrote in his introduction:

> Getting something published is even harder than writing it. It is natural that writers will despair if they do not receive any assistance in delivering their work to others. I am grateful to all the friends who helped to lead *Basain* along the road to publication and especially to Mr. B. B. Gurung and the editor of *Swatantra Nepali* (Free Nepali), Mr. Thakur Chandan Singh. Mr. Kamal Dixit of Sri Darbar, Pulchowk, Lalitpur, took up the burden of publishing it. This was not only a service to literature; it also deepened the friendship that exists between Nepal and Assam, for which I can find no adequate words of thanks. I also express my heartfelt gratitude to the Madan Puraskar Pustakalaya for deciding to print this book.
>
> Finally, if *Basain* has found a place in the readers' hearts, though it be smaller even than a sesame seed, then I shall feel that it has served literature in some measure, and I shall be inspired to publish my other works.

When he began to investigate the possibility of publishing *Basain*, Chettri had only the handwritten manuscript. He first wrote to Thakur Chandan Singh, a well-known Nepali publisher and cultural activist based in Dehra Dun in the Indian Himalaya west of Nepal. Singh advised him to contact the Madan Puraskar Pustakalaya (Madan prize library), an institution in Kathmandu that awarded and still awards a prestigious annual Nepali literary prize. Although the Madan Puraskar Pustakalaya was not engaged in book publication, its founder, Kamal Mani Dixit, wrote to request a copy of the manuscript. Chettri was not particularly interested: "What did I know about who Kamal Dixit was at that time? The distance from Kathmandu to Guahati must be almost 1000 miles!" (1992:38). But the faithful Chatra Bahadur Gurung undertook the laborious task of copying the whole manuscript out by hand and completed it within a week. About one year later, *Basain* was published, and a year after that it was incorporated in the Nepali literature curriculum of Nepal's newly founded Tribhuvan University.

THE SETTING

The novel is set in the hills of far-eastern Nepal, as the author makes clear in his introduction. It was from this region that very large migrations, particularly of people belonging to the Limbu ethnolinguistic group, took place during the nineteenth century after the region had been absorbed into the new Gorkhali state. Nowadays, the Limbus have been marginalized politically in most districts by the Nepali-speaking high Parbatiya castes—the

Bahuns (Brahmans) and Chetris who migrated into the area after the Gorkhali expansion—and by the Newar traders who followed in their wake (see Caplan 1970). Generally, Chetris might therefore be expected to be wealthier than most Limbus, and a stereotypical dispossessed nineteenth-century emigré from far-eastern Nepal would tend to be a Limbu. But Dhan Bahadur Basnet is not a Limbu; he is a Chetri, and the ethnicity of the author is probably a factor here: as a Chetri, he probably felt more confident writing about his own kind. In fact, although there is a mention of a nearby Limbu village and one of the village leaders is a *subba* (traditionally a Limbu title), almost all the characters of the novel appear to be either high-caste Hindus (Bahuns and Chetris) or members of the "low" Parbatiya artisanal castes: Kamis, Damais, and so on.

The historical setting of the story is not made explicit. In his introduction, Chettri explains that he began to write it in 1954 and finished it three years later. One literary scholar, Rajendra Subedi (1996:81), states that the novel sets out to portray the feudal conditions that prevailed in Nepal before the overthrow of the Rana regime in 1950–1951. If one were to hazard a guess, however, one would have to say that the events of the story may be thought of as unfolding at some time roughly contemporaneous with the writing of the novel, although they are still redolent of the fate that befell earlier generations. One feels that Chettri's aim is essentially to portray a conservative social order that has existed for generations. It may be located in time somewhere around the middle of the twentieth century, but one cannot (and need not) be more specific than that.

The novel describes and refers to many aspects of the life of a hill village in eastern Nepal. Its author wrote it for a Nepali readership, not for the foreign reader, and so the text inevitably implies, infers, and assumes a great deal that will not be readily apparent to many non-Nepalis. I have therefore done my best to clarify and explain these references in notes as the story proceeds, drawing where necessary on the published works listed in the bibliography.

Lil Bahadur Chettri modestly states that his portrait of village life may not be wholly reliable. Nonetheless, the agricultural cycle of the Nepali year is richly described and provides the story with its background and context. The foreign reader will therefore benefit from some familiarity with its main features, and the following brief summary is based on an account of the agricultural cycle as it was observed by Philippe Sagant in a Limbu village situated at midaltitude in the hills of eastern Nepal (Sagant 1996:248–77).

The agricultural cycle of each year is conceived of as an annual process of rising and falling, with the arrival of the rains toward the end of Jeth (May–June) or Asar (June–July) as its climactic point. During the months leading up to the rains (Phagun, Chait, Baisakh, corresponding to the period February–May), the weather grows warmer, and farmers plant crops such as maize, wheat, and potatoes. The livestock that has been grazing close to the village through the winter is taken up to higher pastures. When the monsoon breaks, rice and millet seeds are sown close together in the freshly plowed, flooded paddy fields. After these have sprouted into seedlings (usually in Saun [July–August]), they are transplanted farther apart in the paddy fields. As the rains ease during

Bhadau (August–September), the maize crop is harvested, husked, and dried, and the rice and millet crops are weeded. The first rice and millet is harvested during Asoj (September–October) in the run-up to the great annual festival of Dasain. Then, during Kattik (October–November), while fruit and vegetables are abundant, the weather clears, and the livestock begin to return from higher pastures to the fields around the village. During Mangsir (November–December), the weather is bright, but the mornings and nights grow chilly. The big late-rice harvest takes place, barley and wheat are sown, and late millet and lentils are harvested. Pus (mid-December–mid-January) and Magh (mid-January–mid-February) are the coldest and quietest months: the rice is hulled and husked, and straw is stored away. As spring comes around again and the seasons begin once more to "rise," the rain-watered fields are plowed, and the first maize is planted. Altitude is the main factor governing when a given crop is sown, transplanted, and harvested: the greater the altitude, the later the growing season, and of course a crop such as rice can only be grown in fields that can be flooded and are therefore usually in or near the valley bottoms. As Chetris, Dhané and his family are likely to live at a somewhat lower altitude than most Limbus. The village appears to be situated at middle altitude, with irrigable *khet* fields situated in the valley floor (*besi*) below it and forests and pastureland above.

Various types of officials—*subba*, *mukhiya*, and *baidar*—appear in the narrative, and this fictional village would appear to be governed under a rather confusing mixture of systems from different periods. The subba was one of the local officials who had the right to dispense justice in Limbuan (the region of eastern Nepal that the Limbu ethnic group considers its homeland), according to a decree issued in 1883. The mukhiya or village headman was a link between the central government and the community who was mainly responsible for the collection of homestead taxes and other levies but whose jurisdiction also covered most other aspects of village life (Sagant 1996:141; Regmi 1978:71). The baidar was a kind of headman's assistant who had to be literate, even if only barely so, because he needed to read and interpret the Legal Code (*Muluki Ain*) for the headman and assist in the drafting of contracts and petitions.

Mention is made in the novel of a council that is referred to sometimes as the *pancha* and sometimes as the *panchayat*. The panchayat system of national government, which consisted of a pyramidical structure of elected councils from village to national level with the king at its apex, was not established in Nepal until 1962, some five years after this novel was written. Therefore these terms are being used here as Turner defines them in his 1930 Nepali dictionary: as a "committee, jury, body of arbitrators" or "a caste-committee to discuss any matter concerning caste" (359). The panchayat council consisted of the most senior and powerful men of the village and was dominated by the headman and his baidar.

THIS TRANSLATION

The anthropologists and historians whose writings constitute the bulk of the material on Nepal that has been published by foreigners since the country opened to researchers in the 1950s have paid scant attention to the work of Nepali writers. Thus the representations of Nepali society and history that appear in Nepali works of fiction remain little known beyond their Nepali readership. The truism that "literature is a mirror of society" is often quoted in Nepali, but creative literature is of course more aptly described as a lens that may distort an image by playing up particular aspects of a social reality for its own purposes while ignoring others. This it is fully entitled to do, because a novel or a short story is never intended, expected, or required to impart unbiased, factual truths. Nonetheless, the portrayals of socioeconomic issues and processes that may be found in such texts are of great value and interest in themselves. The way a family's dispossession and flight from Nepal are represented in a popular novel such as *Basain* tells us something about the historical fact of migration from the Nepalese hills, as well as revealing an author's attitudes to that fact. Both are significant for an understanding of the relationship between Nepal's past and its present. This was my first reason for translating *Basain*.

A foreign reader who associates South Asian literature with novels written by Booker Prize winners who write only in English may find the characters of this novel—the humble farmer, the rapacious moneylender, the innocent girl, the wily soldier— somewhat stereotypical. My advice to such readers is that they should approach the story in the manner in which they might approach a chronicle or a parable. The remorseless process of Dhané and Maina's impoverishment, exploitation, dispossession, and banishment represents the opening up of a deep division in their society: between those who enjoy some measure of prosperity because they can exploit the poor and those who submit to this exploitation, become increasingly impoverished, and eventually leave. It unfolds against a background in which social relations remain profoundly unequal and are still based on considerations of caste and gender. An anonymous reviewer of an earlier version of this translation wrote that in view of the then-ongoing political crisis in Nepal it seemed strange, at first glance, to consider publishing a novel written in 1957 that was not overtly political. But the reviewer then went on to write that "on further reflection it began to seem highly relevant. *Basain* is a moving story, depicting in wonderful rich detail the round of village life: the daily farmwork and chores, the gossip chain, the weekly market, the limited opportunities, the rapacious rich preying on the poor, and women's particular vulnerabilities. . . . Reading this story could contribute to understanding why poor villagers would join the Maoist cause, if they were given a gun and told they could shoot or drive off Nande and the Baidar on behalf of the revolution, instead of leaving everything they owned."

Moreover, this is a story that has struck a chord in the hearts of hundreds of thousands of Nepali readers since it was first published. In fact, *Basain* is one of a handful of Nepali novels that almost every Nepali reader knows well. Its events and characters are familiar to schoolchildren and their parents alike, and any outsider who cares for the people of Nepal and wishes to understand them better would do well to look into their society through the window this novel provides. In my view it deserves to be better known not only for this reason but also because it is a beautiful, empathetic, poignant story. The style of its telling draws, humbly and without pretension, on the music, intimacy, and wit of the Nepali language, and it succeeds purely on its own terms.

This translation, like all translations, has had to choose between different options at many a juncture, and it is therefore inherently imperfect. In particular, the Nepali used in the dialogue contains many rustic figures of speech, which are difficult to replicate in translation, though I strive to reflect them wherever possible. Also, the novel's characters regularly address one another by using kinship terms instead of personal names, and the translator must decide whether to retain the original Nepali words (*daju, bhai, jetha, didi, kanchi, bhaujyu*, etc.) or whether to translate them ("elder brother," "younger brother," "firstborn son," "elder sister," "last-born daughter," "sister-in-law"). Eventually I opted for the former course of action in most instances, and I have also tried to reflect the fact that the meaning of an epithet such as "Kanchi" can vary slightly, according to who is applying it to whom. I must record my thanks to Indra Bahadur Rai for answering many queries, to Larry Hartsell for sending me a copy of his own translation of this novel, and also to Kamal Dixit, the original publisher, who read an early draft and provided some useful advice.

Michael Hutt
Tring, England

MOUNTAINS PAINTED WITH TURMERIC

◈ 1

This night was not as cold as it usually is in the high hills during the month of Phagun.[1] The sky was overcast, and the cold breeze did not blow from the peaks, so the night was still. Although it was the bright half of the month, all the moon's light could not reach the earth, and there was only just enough light to see by.

From a distance, Dhané Basnet looked as if he were asleep, bundled up from his feet to his head in a dirty quilt that was torn in places. But he was not sleeping. He was trying to set aside the flood of emotions that was tumbling down on him, so that he could welcome the goddess of sleep. But his efforts were all to no avail. One moment he would shut off the flow of thoughts and try to sleep, but the next second those feelings would revive and come back to surround his brain. So Dhané got up, went to the fireplace, plucked out a glowing ember from the ashes, and lit a stub of tobacco wrapped in an *angeri* leaf. As he blew the tobacco smoke out into the room, he sank back into his thoughts. Questions, objections, answers, and then more questions arose one after the other in each corner of his heart.

"The old *baidar*[2] is prepared to give me a buffalo, but he's asking a terribly sharp price—and then of course I have to pledge my plowing oxen as security. If I don't pay off the interest each and every month I'll get no peace at all. 'Four-legged is my wealth; do not ever count it,' they say.[3] If anything goes wrong I'll lose the oxen and everything else as well. But what *could* go wrong? The buffalo's pregnant, and she's already got a sturdy calf. And she gives plenty of milk, too. In a year or two the calf will grow up. And if we get another female calf the next time she gives birth, that will be better still. My little boy will get some milk to wet his throat as well. If we put a little aside for a few days we'll have ghee, and we'll surely make a few annas.[4] That would be enough to pay the interest, and we'll keep the buttermilk. If the maize is good this year I'll use it to pay off half the debt, and we'll just live on millet." His thoughts raced by like a powerful torrent. When the tobacco was all gone, Dhané, "the wealthy one,"[5] wrapped himself in his quilt again. Half the night had passed already, and he yawned.

Dhan Bahadur Basnet is a young man: he has just turned twenty-five. His frame attests to the mountain air and the nutritious food of his homeland, but his handsome face is always darkened by clouds of worry, like black clouds sullying a clear night. He has just one life companion: his wife, Maina, who supports him through his times of sorrow and rejoices when he is happy. In Maina's lap there plays the star of Dhané's future, a three-year-old boy. The family also includes a girl of fourteen or fifteen, Dhané's youngest sister, Jhumavati, whose marriage Dhané has not yet arranged because of his financial difficulties. The boat of Dhané's household bobs along bearing its little family of four, facing many storms on the unfathomed seas of the world.

Dhané's crisis may be likened to the black clouds and moon of this night. The moon wants to cut through the net of clouds and spread light throughout the world, making it blissful in the cool soft joy it provides. But it is unable to do so: the clouds have reduced its light to nothing. Dhané wants to burst through the net of his money problems and bring his little family happiness and the cool shade of peace. He longs to restore the foundations of the roofpoles and posts that the termites of his debts to the moneylenders have made rickety. For that he has relied on his industry and labor. He works hard, he is industrious. For every four cowries[6] he is willing to lay down a bet on the last breath of his life. But his hardships do not change.

The rotting posts of his house just go on rotting. Like mist rising up to join the clouds, the land owners and moneylenders of the village add to his problems. The sharp interest rates they charge, the way they snatch the security pledged if a promise is broken: in Dhané's life these are like the blows of staves on a man who is already unconscious. But despite all this he has not admitted defeat. He hides his sorrows and goes on treading the path of labor.[7]

3 ◇

"Hariram! The price of the buffalo is 120 rupees, the interest must be delivered to Hariram's house at the end of every month. And listen! If you are late by even a day during the months that you owe money to Hariram, I tell you I'll remove the oxen and the buffalo from your shed! There, what do you say? Make a mark with your thumb on the agreement." So said the baidar, who wore a fresh mark of white sandalwood paste on his brow.

The baidar was an old man, a firm traditionalist who paid great attention to matters of purity and touchability. He ate nothing that had not been prepared by his own Bahun cook. So that the name of Ram might always be on his lips, he sprinkled everything he said with his pet word, "Hariram." His mornings passed in ritual and scripture, and he considered the giving of alms and feasts to Bahuns to be the highest duty. But he was always on his guard when the poor and suffering of the neighborhood came to borrow something petty. He did not forget to crank up the interest when someone borrowed a rupee or two, and the wages for all his hard work were earned by extracting high rates of interest from his creditors. Dhané knew the baidar well. Even though he knew that dealing with him was like setting his own house alight, he held his peace and made his mark on the paper.

It was time to let the livestock out to graze. The farm workers were making their way down to the fields, carrying baskets and *ghum*s.[8] Dhané came back to his yard, dragging the little calf behind him. The buffalo brought up the rear, bellowing as it came. Maina hurriedly scattered a handful of hay to one side of the yard, and the buffalo sampled it casually.

◈ 4

Dhané expected to profit from the buffalo in every way. "After a year or two my bad days will be over and my good days will begin," he thought. But if things always worked out as they were envisaged, no one in the world would ever have blamed fate for anything. It was only about two weeks since Dhané had bought the buffalo. He came out that morning to milk it, carrying a milk

pail with a little butter smeared on its rim. He went over to untie the calf, but then he saw that it was lying with its legs spread out and that one of its legs was quivering. He had tethered the calf in a hurry the previous evening, and when he saw it like this he nearly lost his senses. He told Maina and then went up the hill to call Kahila Dhami from the big house.[9] The *dhami* came quickly, and when he had fingered the grains of rice in the tray for a long time he said, "It seems that Bankalé has got it.[10] You just light incense for the deities of the house, and I'll conduct an exorcism."

It was just time to light the lamps in the village houses. The cowherds were busy laying out feed and spreading litter for their livestock. Over by the stream the crickets made the air resound with the music of their ensemble, as if some musicians from the city were playing their *tanpuras*. Down below, Telu Magar's dog barked monotonously. Dhané was standing beside the calf, his eyes brimming with tears. The calf turned its eyes toward him and gave a cry of utter misery, as if it wanted to tell him in its mute infant's language that this was the last hour of its life. Dhané wiped his tear-filled eyes with the hem of his shirt and sat down beside the calf. "Go now, mother, go happily. May your soul find joy in the other place." The calf gave one strong kick and then gave up its breath, as if it were obeying his command. At milking time, the buffalo kicked out, brandished its horns, and jumped around, and Dhané was unable to touch it.

It was Phagun, and the fields were empty and bare. Several farmers had just begun their plowing. Dhané had let his buffalo out onto his dry field, and at midday he lay sunning himself on some straw on the open roof of his lean-to. Just then, Leuté Damai arrived in a foul temper.[11] Leuté was very wealthy. He reaped a profit from sewing for the whole village, and he also had plenty of fields of his own, so he did not need to defer to anyone. Dhané climbed down from the roof, and Leuté saluted him, lifting one hand to his brow: "*Jadau*, Saheb," he said.[12] "Have you let your buffalo loose? It's been through my field, and it hasn't left a single stem of my buckwheat standing. If my patrons let their stock wander out like this as if they were bulls,[13] what will be left of me? Come with me and see the damage your buffalo has done!"

"It can't have been in there for long; it was in my own field just now!" said Dhané.

"I don't know anything more about it, but I'm going to get the *mukhiya* to fine you for this. You'll have to pay whatever he decides."

"All right, all right, there's no need to get so excited, Damai! If it's destroyed your crop I'll repay you!"

"Do you think you can still talk down to me like that when your buffalo has ruined me? I'm going to the mukhiya right now!" Leuté strode off. Very soon he returned with the mukhiya and several other men, and they went over to Leuté's buckwheat field, taking Dhané with them.

There was a ravine between Dhané's and Leuté's fields. The far wall of the ravine, on Leuté's side, was very high, and cattle and buffaloes were unable to climb into Leuté's field. But Dhané's buffalo had followed the ravine right down to the main path and had then gone around to get into Leuté's large terraced field, where it had destroyed roughly half the buckwheat. It was resolved that Dhané should pay a fine of three *mohar*s.[14] He was made to promise to pay within ten days, and a written record was made of this. When they had secured Dhané's mark on the paper, the mukhiya and the other men returned to their homes.

Haay, the ways of fate are strange! One afternoon in the burning sun of Chait[15] the buffalo came staggering into the cowshed. Dhané came down from the yard and was about to pat it when he noticed that it bore some bruises, which he guessed had been caused by some blows from a stick. He was speechless. But what could a poor man like Dhané do? Slowly he muttered, "Who hit you like this? You must have got into someone's crops. That's just how it is." The buffalo's womb had been injured, and four days later its calf was stillborn.

5 ◇

The sun's yellow rays fell on the peaks of the next range of mountains, and they looked as if some artist had painted them with turmeric. A cool evening breeze had begun to blow, and out in the alleyways the herders were calling as they brought in their animals. Some birds were creating a din up in the juniper trees and chir pines; it was as if they were singing at the tops of their voices to rejoice at being all together. A day in the month of Bhadau:[16] all around one could see nothing but maize, which obscured the narrow houses of the village. Maize grew on both sides of the main path, and those who came and went along it could not be seen from a distance.

Someone was coming down the hillside toward the village. In such a place his attire was a thing of wonder. He wore belted military khaki trousers, and a *khukuri* knife hung at his side. The collar of his white shirt was out over his black coat, and on his feet he wore a pair of red shoes. On his head there was a black pointed cap, in his hand there was a walking stick, and from his shoulder there hung a bag with several rugs rolled up in a belt on top of it. On his young, fair-complexioned face there shone for all to see the arrogant look of a soldier.

There was a spring on the main path above Dhané's house. Previously there had been no water there, but one year during the rains water suddenly burst forth. The spring never dried up after that, even when winter came, and the villagers got together and laid down a pointed rock over which the water could run, making the sound "chararar." They called it the "waterfall spring," and those who lived nearby drew their water from it.

The young man reached the spring and stopped to gaze at a girl who was there. She was just like a budding flower! He had seen many such flowers in the city, all smothered in scent and powder. He had seen many young beauties wrapped in silk blouses and blue saris, and he had thought them real nymphs. But could he have imagined such a flower in an ordinary hill village, wearing a common calico skirt, a dirty white cotton waistband, and a blouse torn in three places? He had not known this until today, when he saw such a one there before him. The only difference was that those flower buds in the towns watered their roots themselves, while nature itself watered this one. In the town, they wore rouge and fake roses, but the goddess of nature had endowed this one with every adornment. In the town, the whole environment had been artificial, but here everything was just as it should be.

The young man stared. That blossoming young body and everything that was on it attracted his heart: the little ring in her nostril and the stud in her shapely nose, the rings on her ears, the coral necklace that hung down from her neck to her breast, the waistband that held a fold of her sari up above her slender waist, the cloth she wore over the back of her head to cover her hair, her fair face. . . .

The innocent village girl had just finished washing her hands and feet. As she straightened her back, her eyes met a more forceful gaze. The young man did not even blink. Each was sizing the other up. But how strange! The same look was not in both pairs of eyes. The young man's showed desire and romance, while in the girl's there glimmered only simplicity and a kind of attraction that came from her heart. Before long, an expression of natural womanly modesty appeared on the girl's face, and sweat glistened on her brow. She lowered her eyes, sat down to one side of the spring, and began to wash out the various implements her family used in religious rituals. Still standing right there, the soldier was trying to decide how to speak to her. "How should I address her? It's not right to call someone 'Nani' when she is a grown-up young woman. Shall I call her 'Bahini'? No, I think I'll address her without using any name. . . ."[17]

"Hey," he said, "can I get some water to drink here?"

"Of course you can, don't you think there's enough water? Can't you see how big the spring is?"

The girl was busy washing a pot. The youth rinsed out his mouth and then drank from the spring. After he had drunk his fill, he squatted on the bank to rest for a while. He took a cigarette from a packet of Passing Show, lit it, and then blew the smoke out over the girl's head, where it disappeared. "Where does this path lead?" he asked.

"I've never really been farther than Limbugaon.[18] I don't know where it ends up."

"How far would Limbugaon be now?"

"Oh, still about two *kos*, I suppose."[19]

"Ay, it's a long way away. I'm tired out! I don't think I'll manage to walk two *kos* today."

The girl became curious. She glanced up at the youth, then looked down again right away.

"Is that where you're going?" she asked.

"Yes, that's where my home is. I haven't been there for years. I've almost forgotten the way." After a moment he said, "Your home is here, I suppose?"

He had addressed her using the politest word for "you," and the girl blushed.[20] A little flustered, she said quietly, "Yes . . . it's that house down there."

The youth blurted out a question. "If I had to call you by your name, what name would I use?"

The girl was rather taken aback. She realized that things were going a little too far and was ever so slightly annoyed with the youth for his forwardness. But her anger quickly cooled. "I've no idea what you'd call me," she said rather seriously. "Others call me Jhuma."

The soldier understood her attitude and was not bold enough to ask her anything else. Jhuma finished scrubbing and began to rinse the pots in the spring. Without saying anything more, the youth got up and went slowly on his way. Jhuma turned once to look back at him. She could not understand why, but she felt as if her heart was walking away with him.

6 ◈

The sun had set, but it was not yet completely dark. Jhuma put all the pots into a basket, picked up the filled water jar, and took her leave of the waterfall spring. She was not usually especially happy to see the maize overhanging both sides of the path; most of the time she considered it a nuisance. But today it was as if the plants were sitting beside the path to welcome her, and she saw something special in them. Today she felt as if something novel had touched her life.

When Jhuma stepped into the courtyard at home her face took on an expression that was a mixture of hope, surprise, and shy pleasure, along with a little tinge of pain. She saw that the same person she had met earlier was seated on a mat he had spread out on her verandah and was talking to her brother,

Dhané, who was sitting on a bedstead. She glanced at them and went quickly indoors.

Dhané was engrossed in their conversation.

"Oh, so you must be in a government post, is that right?"

"Yes, I suppose that's what you must call it. You have to pass the time somehow, you know!"

"How long is it since you went abroad?"

"Oh, I've been abroad since I was young. I can have been only about fourteen when I left the hills, and now I've been in the army for three years. At first I suffered a lot to make ends meet. I herded other people's cows and buffaloes, I did any work I could. Suddenly I found myself in the army—it was just a matter of luck. Now let's just say that in a sense I'm really quite comfortably off."

"That's right, once you've joined the army, what else do you need to look for? It's wonderful, isn't it! And who do you have back here in the hills?"

"No one at all, really. There's my *dai*, the son of my father's younger brother.[21] He will have children by now, I expect." The soldier stretched out his legs and looked out across the yard. "It's gotten very dark. I'd better be off."

"Ah, we are Chetris, too; we can eat together," Dhané said casually.[22] "Just eat with us and sleep here tonight. Why go to Limbugaon now? It's too far when night is falling. It would be fine if you set out in the morning."

"Yes, you're right. It's dark, and I'm tired. Perhaps I should stay till tomorrow."

"That's right. Why hurry? You'll be home in time for the morning meal!"

7 ◇

Nowadays all the housework falls on Jhuma's shoulders. The baby makes many demands on Maina, so she can't offer to help with many of the domestic chores. She helps her husband's sister to wash the pots and to mill and pound the grain. Otherwise, all the cooking and serving of food is Jhuma's responsibility.

When she had finished preparing the food, Jhuma went and sat beside Maina. "Bhaujyu, the food's ready.[23] Would you serve the meal today?"

Maina took Jhuma's chin in her hand and lifted her head so that they looked each other in the eye. "The one who cooks the food should serve it herself. Will you issue orders like this when you are married and you have your own home?" After a moment she said, "Go, my pretty child, give your brother and his guest some water and put the rice on their plates, while I finish plaiting this rope."

Jhuma would laugh and joke with her sister-in-law, but she respected and honored her as if she were her mother, and she could not disobey her. She made herself get up and fill the pitcher from the water jar, then went outside. She approached the soldier with the pitcher in her hand, bowing her head as low as she possibly could. The soldier tried to look thirstily into her eyes, but in the dim light that filtered out to the edge of the verandah from the house he could not see her face. He could only see her head, covered with a veil. Jhuma's heart was pounding away, and she did not try to look at the soldier. She just put the water down next to him and went back indoors.

Dhané and the soldier washed their hands and feet and came in to sit beside the raised earthen hearth. Jhuma's head was bowed, and as she pushed a plate of rice in front of the soldier her hand trembled. The lamp in a niche in the wall was burning down. In the gloom Jhuma glanced once at the soldier's face and found that his eyes were on her, too, so she quickly looked away. Maina rose and turned up the lamp, and the room became bright again.

After the meal, the stranger went out and lay down on a bed on the verandah. When they had finished their other tasks, Jhuma and Maina went off to the granary store with a basket of maize, and soon the grinding sound of the millstone fell on the recumbent soldier's ears. The dark night was completely still. The distant insect noise was drowned out by the "gharr, gharr" sound of the millstone as it turned. It sounded as if the earth were taking its final breaths. In the midst of peaceful nature a sweet gentle voice began to sing its own song, a *sangini*.[24] Nature came alive in the song and the atmosphere completely changed.

Jhuma sings a sangini, and her voice is thin but sweet. It is an old custom for village women to sing a sangini as they grind grain, and Maina is very fond of it. She is always the one who begins the song, and Jhuma always takes it up behind her. But today, she does not know why, Jhuma is impatient to show off the sweetness of her voice. She waits for ages for her sister-in-law to begin to sing, but then she can wait no longer, and she begins the song herself. This day her voice comes out filled with life; something new fills her throat. Soon Maina joins in, too. The sangini had been smiling with Jhuma's voice, and now it begins to laugh. That sound truly possesses the power to melt rocks as it issues out into the night in that silent village.

And the soldier is really only a man, an ordinary man. He had heard sangini songs during his childhood, before he left for Mugalan.[25] In Mugalan he had never had a chance to hear a sangini, but today, after so many years, he became reacquainted with his own village song. His ears heard nothing else, and he felt greatly moved. He thought to himself, "I must get up, I must follow the ripples of music that come from that voice, and when I have found their source I must fall at her feet and surrender myself to her." His heart flew here and there, here and there, with the waves of the sangini, and a strange vision danced before his eyes. At one point he even decided that he would get up and go to Jhuma. But then he considered that there was someone else there with Jhuma and decided that it would not be right to approach her in the night like that. In the end he lay where he was, restraining his emotions. After a long while the singing and the "gharr, gharr" of the millstone both fell still. The soldier covered his face and tried to sleep.

It was his custom to rise very early, and the next morning he got up and prepared to set out. He bade Dhané farewell and came out into the yard, and there before him, near the door to the granary, stood Jhuma. They looked steadily at each other for a few seconds. Both pairs of eyes were saying: "If we live long enough, we will meet again," but each was unsure of the other. The stranger went on his way, feeling as if he had left an empty shadow somewhere. Jhuma returned to the house with a heavy heart, feeling as if one of her limbs had been removed.

◇ 8

Teej had just taken its leave of the women of Nepali society, and now the Sorah Shraddha arrived, a sign that Dasain was near.[26] Everyone was assembling the things they needed to celebrate Dasain. In almost every villager's house the sweet sound of "Jay Devi Bhairavi!" could be heard.[27] The herdsmen who gathered at the cowherders' huts sang the sweet tune of "Malashri" in unison instead of their usual songs.[28] Everyone seemed happy at the arrival of Dasain, and why should they not, after all? These are two days during which loads can be laid aside and some rest can be taken, in lives that are oppressed all year round by the burden of daily labor. And the feast also gives people an opportunity to meet close friends and relations they have not seen for years and to shed tears of joy as they are reunited with them.

Outside, the whole world is enjoying itself. Dhané Basnet takes part in the general cheerfulness, but his smile sits on his lips and spreads no further. Instead, a fierce fire burns in his heart. So far he has managed to pay the old baidar only two months' interest. Whenever the baidar passes his house on his various comings and goings he stops his horse for a moment and calls,

"Oh, Dhané! Why haven't you kept your word to Hariram? How much does the interest come to now, do you not know? When you took away Hariram's buffalo you were weeping and wailing with gratitude. But now you don't even know Hariram! I was out of my mind, why on earth did I give the buffalo to someone like you? If you don't send Hariram's interest in a few days' time, I'll empty out your cowshed, do you understand?"

Dhané is infuriated as he listens, but he is helpless—what can he do? He keeps his head bowed and says nothing.

Meanwhile, there was the problem of Dasain to consider. Everyone had to have a special new set of clothes. There wasn't a grain of rice, and nothing to eat beside maize.[29] These were the many problems that Dhané faced.

Today Dhané ate hurriedly and left the house at dawn. He did not return until late that night. Maina hurried to give him some water to wash himself with, so that he could eat. When he had eaten, Dhané lay down on his bed. Maina finished her chores and then filled a wooden pot with oil and sat down at his feet. Jhuma was already asleep on her own bed. Gently, Maina began to massage Dhané's feet; this was virtually a daily task for her. Dhané's gaze fell on Maina's simple face, and suddenly happiness flowed into his grieving heart, which filled with a peculiar compassion for her. He thought to himself: "Poor Maina! How hard she works all day, but she doesn't get even a handful of anything good to eat. She is a mother, but even when she had just given birth there was nothing good to give her. So many feasts have come and gone, but I could never afford to give her a single piece of nice jewelry, except for the nose stud and earrings that were made for her when we married. But even so, how content she is! She always attends to my troubles, She bears the burden of the whole house. It is a matter of fate: karma joined this flower to a poor man like me."

He sat up slowly and took hold of one of Maina's hands as she massaged his feet. In a voice full of pity and love he said, "Oh, that will do, how much longer can you go on doing that? You're tired, sleep now."

Maina had been a little afraid of her husband's grave manner up to now and had not dared to speak. But when she heard his loving words her face lit up. Slowly, she released her hand from his and said brightly, "Am I doing it because you ordered me to? Should I stop because you say it's enough or carry on until you do? No, I do this because it pleases me!"

Dhané smiled along with her. "All right, then, if that's so, just do as you please. Stay awake all night!"

After a while, Maina touched Dhané's feet with her head and stood up. She put the oil pot back in its place and returned to Dhané's side. She ran her soft hand through his hair and asked him, "Where were you all afternoon? Did you have some work to do in the village?"

At this his expression become grave again. After a few moments he replied, "Where do you think I went? I went to see if Budhé Kami would give me thirty rupees.[30] Fifteen to plug the baidar's mouth and the other fifteen to get us through this Dasain: that was the idea. But why would the damned blacksmith give it to me? He just kept putting me off all day. Dasain is nearly here, and I've not bought clothes for anyone; how are we are going to manage, eh?" He heaved a long sigh as soon as he had finished speaking.

Maina calmed her husband. "Do you need to worry so much about it? The girl may need fresh clothes, but the rest of us still have last year's. Goats are fetching a good price in the village, so sell that piebald one. You'll get twenty rupees for it, won't you? The white one's kid will be enough for the household to eat. There's a market the day after tomorrow; the girl can go with her friends and get a skirt and blouse. She's dying to go, anyway."

"How can I sell a goat from your *peva*?[31] You struggled so hard to rear those two kids, what will we do if we get rid of them, too? I wanted to add to your peva, but that's come to naught."

"My peva? Who do I have to hide it from? I have no sisters-in-law to envy me! I swear it, what does my peva matter, compared to my husband and son?"

Dhané was choked when he heard Maina say this. Although he was poor in material terms, God had given him this priceless jewel. It was many times better to be a beggar with a life companion like Maina than to be as rich as Kubera[32] but have no one to share your sorrows. Unable to suppress his joy, Dhané said, "How hard it is to understand the games the gods play! Although I am poor, the Lord gave me a wife that not even a king could get! I am poor, but I am fortunate to have a wife like you!"

"That will do, there's no need to flatter me!" Maina protested.

Then the child in Maina's bed grew restless and whimpered in his dreams. Maina got up from Dhané's bed and laid down beside the child to soothe him back to sleep.

Today is the day of the Sunday market.[33] Ever since the sun came up, women, children, and all the people of the villages have been walking toward the hill on which the market is held. Today, people from as far as a day's walk away gather to buy and sell on this hill. And the importance of the market for these villagers does not end with trade—this is also a place for catching up with people you have to meet. Many people also come to the market to collect papers and letters brought there for them by others, or to pass on a letter they themselves have brought from some office or other, and for many other such things. The market is held here once every two weeks, and it is a vital thing for the villagers.

Early this morning, Jhuma bathed at that waterfall spring that we already know. A second young woman arrived, carrying a pitcher on her hip. She looked at Jhuma. "*Aayu!*" she said. "How can Kanchi Didi[34] bear to pour water over herself first thing in the morning? Is your body made of iron?"

"Oh, it's you, you *mori!*[35] But you must be here for a bath as well! Are you going to the market?"

"Well, I might be. But even if I am, who do I have to show myself off to that I should bathe so early? Who have you got at the market to do yourself up for?"

"We'll look later on, won't we, when it's time to set out! We'll look to see who's been making themselves up! We'll find out then!"

"Yes, that's right, *didi*, we certainly will! Who else is going to the market?"

"Just you, probably! Who else do I need? If we go in a crowd we'll never be able to have any fun. Let's just go on our own, just us two, all right?"

"Yes, all right! I'll come to your place. Make sure you get away early."

"All right, Thuli. Are you going empty-handed, or are you taking some rice to sell?"

"Where would I get rice? There's a *pathi* of big soybeans, I'm taking that. How about you?"[36]

"I'm not taking anything. My brother gave me some money to buy clothes. I have to look for a skirt."

"Right, don't be slow! I'll be along very soon."

Thuli's pitcher was full, and she carried it off up the hill. Jhuma got dressed and began to scrub her pots.

◈ ◈ ◈

Jhuma and Thuli set out in good time. Up by the copse of alder trees, Moté Karki was dragging three stout *khasi* goats up the slope.[37] Jhuma and Thuli hurried to catch up with him.

"Karki *daju*'s having such a struggle to get his goats to market," said Thuli. "The market will have upped and gone by the time he gets there!"

"Come on, come on," Karki urged his goats, then he looked at the girls. "Ay, what market will we ever reach? *Lu, lu*! Drive them up from behind, Thuli. They're giving me a lot of grief; they just refuse to walk."

Thuli picked up a little stick and began to hit the goats with it, and they quickened their pace a little.

"At last the great bulls walk to meet their end!" Karki heaved a long sigh.

"He'll have to give me half his profits now that I've helped him so much," laughed Thuli. "It looks as if you've decided to empty the village and drive everyone's goats to market!"

"I don't steal them from their pens, you know!" Karki retorted. "You people come and ask me to buy them from you, so what are you telling me now?"

Jhuma had not spoken all this time: she did not talk to Karki very much. Karki, too, behaved most respectfully toward her and never teased her or joked with her. Jhuma gestured to Thuli and said, "Let's go on, Thuli, we've stopped for long enough. Karki will bring them along slowly."

Jhuma and Thuli went on ahead. "Keep going!" Thuli shouted to Karki.

"All right! See you at the market this evening!" Karki went back to shouting at his goats.

Karki was very fat, so he had the nickname Moté, "Fatty." His practice was simply to buy goats from the village and sell them for some small profit at the market. He also owned a fair amount of *khet* and *bari* land.[38] His parents had died when he was young, and he had no brothers or sisters. Nor had he married, so he had neither worries nor sorrows. He had accumulated a little money, but he was not one of those who become so avaricious that they would kill to earn more. "Wealth is what's left over after food and clothes have been bought": this was his maxim. He helped out everyone in the village with chores from time to time, and he was hugely popular among the women of the village. He thoroughly enjoyed joining in and helping them with jobs such as threshing, setting up looms to weave rugs, cleaning and sorting vegetables, and so on. So, if there was a job to be done the village women would think of him. If someone had cooked something a little special they would send out for Karki. Karki did not often cook for himself. He would eat, or be persuaded to eat, wherever there was a gathering in the village. Although his face was not particularly handsome or cheerful, Karki's heart was pure. He wished no one ill, and he was drawn to Jhuma because of her loveliness and simplicity. Many different kinds of feelings for Jhuma played in him, and he truly loved her from his heart. But he had not yet revealed this to her; neither had he been able to broach the subject with her brother. It was only to one or two close friends that he had said, "If they let me I'd marry her, that Kanchi from down the hill."[39]

Karki behaved shyly with Jhuma because of this, but from a distance he did all he could to make her happy. Seeing that Karki was shy, Jhuma behaved shyly with him, too, and did not speak to him very often. If she had to say anything, she spoke well of him. "Karki's a useful man," she would say, but otherwise she took very little notice of him.

A cold breeze blew toward Jhuma and Thuli as they drew near to the Sunday market. Soon they could hear a vague murmur of voices coming from the far side of the ridge, and as they crested the hill they began to see the people who were attending it.

A lot higher up and farther away, huge white boulders could be seen in the middle of a sparse stretch of forest. There was a long stretch of pasture, higher in the middle and dropping away at both sides. It was on this hilltop that all the villages had their grand bazaar. The paths came from all around—east, west, north, and south—and all came together at this spot.[40]

Once they had arrived, Thuli sat down to one side of the path and spread out her stall of soybeans. Jhuma walked off, saying, "I'll just have a look around, I'll be back soon."

Because Dasain was near, everything cost double its normal price. Cloth that usually cost eight annas a foot couldn't even be touched for less than twelve annas. Jhuma wandered past many stalls. Cloth and saris had been brought to the market to be sold for various sums, but the prices were terribly sharp. There was no question of paying less than a rupee per foot, even for something ordinary, and she would need ten feet for a sari. Eventually, she just bought an ordinary red embroidered skirt for eight rupees. She had just taken it from the stallkeeper and was about to walk away when her eyes met those of someone she knew. Pleasure and shyness rose and sank in her heart, because before her she saw the

soldier, who was watching her intently. Her heart beat more quickly, and her feet would not carry her forward. But she did not have the nerve to turn and run away, so she just stood there, rooted to the spot. Meanwhile the soldier took two steps forward and asked her, "What's the matter, don't you recognize me?"

At last a little courage entered her. Raising her head a little, she replied, "Yes, of course, why wouldn't I?"

"Are you well?" was the soldier's second question.

Jhuma fumbled for a reply for ages. Perhaps it was because she had not understood his question properly. After a while she just said, "Yes."

Then the soldier said, "I suppose you've come to do some shopping, have you? But there's nothing here like the things you can get in a real bazaar."[41]

The veil of Jhuma's shyness had been drawn well aside by now, and she felt wholly confident. She looked at the soldier and said, "You'll have searched around like you did on recruit,[42] but this is hardly the same! They say that in Mungalan there are brilliant things to see!"

"Ay, what tales I could tell you of that!" The soldier took a handkerchief from his pocket and wiped his face. "There are electric lights so bright it seems like the sun is shining in the night. And the shops aren't out on open hillsides like this! The bazaar stretches as far as you can see—proper big roads with cars, trams, and rickshaws running along them. You don't have to walk a step, a rickshaw will always run you along. That's how it is there. I was fed up when I realized how things were here."

Jhuma was very surprised by what he said. She could not understand much of it, either. The little mind of this innocent girl, who had never left her village, tried to picture it. "What's it like, Mungalan?" She pondered over this for a while.

"Let's go and talk down in that dip," said the soldier. "All this market noise is deafening me."

Jhuma did not object, and the pair of them walked away from the bazaar toward a nearby hollow. When the sounds of the market were in the distance they sat down in a corner of the field. For a moment neither spoke. Now that he found Jhuma beside him, the soldier's spirits were flying high. He stared without blinking at her loveliness. Finding him staring at her, Jhuma was gripped by her natural shyness again. She began to find the silence unbearable, and so she reopened the conversation.

"When do you go back to Mungalan?"

"Who knows?" the soldier answered casually, his contemplation interrupted. "I'll stay two or three months, I suppose. I've been granted some leave."

Again there was silence between them for a long while. The soldier wanted to ask her something, but he hesitated. Then he plucked up his courage and asked her, "Are you married yet?"

The question made Jhuma blush. She turned her head away and looked at the ground. Then in a small voice she said, "There's no *sindur* in my hair, and I'm not wearing a bead necklace, can't you see?"[43]

The soldier hesitated, then put on a cheerful expression. "Oh! I hadn't thought of that!"

"I really want to ask you something," the soldier said after a pause. "Will you be *naraz*?"[44]

Jhuma looked at him. "What's *naraz*? I can't understand the things you say!"

The soldier chuckled. "What I mean is, will you be angry?" He used the formal pronoun.

"Why should I be? Ask me! But in our village people don't address people younger than themselves as *tapai*. I feel very odd when you call me *tapai*."

"So how should I address you?"

"Use *timi* of course! I am younger than you."

"Oh, *accha*, from now on I'll call you *timi*."[45]

The conversation faltered, but then Jhuma revived it. "What was it you wanted to ask? You didn't ask it, did you?"

"Well, I've been trying to decide whether to ask you or not. . . . Jhuma, after I first saw you I couldn't forget you. I've seen you so many times in my dreams. Will you come with me to Mugalan?"

Jhuma did not pay much attention to the rest of what he had said, because his final words, "Will you come with me to Mugalan?" had had such an effect on her. She was engrossed in her vision of golden Mugalan. But soon she recalled her situation, her place and time. A picture of the poverty of her home danced before her eyes. "Who's going to let me go to Mugalan?" she said sadly. "Why would a little corpse like me ever have such good fortune?"

The soldier felt a little hope enter him. "Ay, it can be arranged, you know! You only have to want it!"

Their conversation was interrupted by the sound of loud shouts from the bazaar, and they walked back together. Two drunks had begun a quarrel, and a crowd had gathered around them to watch the fun. The soldier bought a fine shawl, folded a comb and some thread inside it, and placed it in Jhuma's hand. She protested and tried to refuse to take it, but he insisted, and eventually she had to accept. As they parted, the soldier asked her, "When will we meet again?"

"Won't you come to ride the swing at Dasain? Everyone from your village does. We'll meet then," said Jhuma.[46]

"Fine," said the soldier.

Moté Karki had sold his goats and was coming toward them. When he saw Jhuma talking to a soldier he had not seen before he was curious, but he turned away without speaking to them. Jhuma took her leave of the soldier and went back to Thuli.

◈ **11**

There are streams to either side; between them a high ridge rises, and from the two ravines the "kulululu" sound of the running water that bursts from sources higher up can be heard. These streams bring life to the khet fields in the valley below. Directly beyond the ridge, at a distance of three furlongs, a ritual is to be performed at a sacrificial site.[47] On the rock a buffalo bull will be sacrificed on the eighth day of Dasain. Here and there on the ridge there are a few alder trees and ordinary ferns, bitter-leaves,[48] shrubs, and bushes. In the middle a rotary swing has been erected; this is shared by the three or four villages that lie on the hillsides that drop away from the ridge.

The full moon is shining as bright as the sun; the only thing it lacks is warmth. The whitewashed houses on the far hillside are clearly visible. There is a lot of noise around the swing:

"Yes, Kancha, come here and have a go, won't you?"

"Ay, Jethi, get down now, you've been around lots of times!"

"She's going to fall on her head, see how she's trembling?"

Everyone is engrossed in the fun. But Jhuma and the soldier are a little way from the noisy crowd, sitting under an alder tree and enjoying the beauty of the full moon. So far they have not been able to express all their feelings. Jhuma is more afraid than shy. Guilt, a sense of sin, and her fear of her brother force her to bundle up her emotions inside her. And she is a village girl: what right does she have to make an independent expression of her affection? Her overriding duty is to massage the legs of the man with whose shawl her guardians bind her.[49] But why does the soldier hesitate? Why do his lips tremble whenever he is about to say something? Is it so unpleasant for him to express to his beloved the love that is boiling up in his heart?

The autumn could not bear to see the moon smiling like this, unveiled. The clouds drew a thin veil over it so that its face was covered. The soldier gathered all his courage and slowly took hold of Jhuma's hand. This was the first time he had touched her. Jhuma started and looked apprehensively at him, but the soldier had no time to consider Jhuma's feelings. Slowly, he moved closer to her. She shifted away a little, trying not to let him notice. "Jhuma," he said in a tremulous voice, "Jhuma, will you marry me?"

The question came out of his mouth, but he did not know what he was saying. The sensation he was experiencing, if it had come out in words, would have been expressed quite differently. As soon as he asked his question, Jhuma turned her face from him and moved a little farther away. Slowly she removed her hand from his. An apprehensive expression appeared clearly on her face, mixed with worry and fear. It was not because the soldier's question had frightened her. It was because for some reason she saw in it the cloudy water of a dirty stream, rather than the pure water of a waterfall. She felt that she wanted to escape from this situation. She stood up and looked at the soldier. Then she said gravely, "It doesn't matter what I say, you'd have to go and talk to my daju."

The soldier was put out by the change in Jhuma's mood and by her answer to his question. But right away he grasped the situation. "What's the matter? Are you angry or something?"

"Why should I be angry? It is very late, and my friends are getting ready to leave. I am going now."

The soldier did not object, and he stood up, too. He told Jhuma that he would come the next day, then set off for home by himself. Jhuma rejoined her party. They were still keen to continue playing on the swing, and they were all taken up with their game.

When they had finished with the swing and were climbing back up the hill, the second stage of the night was already passing.

Karki was walking behind Jhuma. He came up beside her and said, "Sister, I didn't see you riding on the swing even once tonight!"

"Oh, who needs to ride on the swing? There's no point in it! I only came because my friend was so keen to."

"Are you too scared to?"

"Scared? What of? I just don't want to ride on the swing, it's pointless!"

"Kanchi, who's that soldier? I've been seeing him talking to you ever since the other day." Karki spoke slowly, in a sorrowful, helpless voice.

Jhuma was cross with Karki for asking this. She found it intolerable. "What! Did you come just to see who I was talking to? Do you lose your caste just from chatting to someone?"

"Why are you so angry?" Karki said meekly. "I didn't say there was anything wrong with chatting, I just asked you who the man was."

Karki's humility made Jhuma ashamed of her harsh reaction. This was the first time in her life she had ever spoken sharply to him. Mortified, she told him, "He lives in Limbugaon, he says. He stayed a night in our house on his way home from the army."

"Don't mix with him so much," said Karki. "It doesn't do to trust these soldier corpses." The words burst out of his mouth although he tried to stop them.

"*Chi*! How suspicious you are, Karki daju! He's not that kind of soldier; he's like a god although he's only a man. If you don't believe me, just talk to him tomorrow and you'll find out!" Jhuma blurted this out. Karki was alarmed by Jhuma's trust in the soldier, but he kept his feelings to himself.

◇ 12

Winter strode slowly up like a blemished incarnation, determined to ruin the whole lovely garden that autumn had prepared. A cold wind had begun to blow in the mornings, and it was increasingly rare for the sun to appear before midday. Dhané had fed his buffalo and oxen, and he was sitting on the wall of the stall, smoking tobacco from a bamboo pipe. Suddenly he noticed some people approaching in the distance. He was so alarmed, it was as if the ground, the wall, the cow pens, everything was spinning around him. It was the old baidar and the mukhiya, and they were approaching with several other villagers. Dhané climbed down, welcomed the visitors, and seated them in a suitable place at the house.

The mukhiya addressed Dhané: "Jetha, you took something from the moneylender, then you did not know what you had to do. This, this, how can this be? Count out Baidar Saheb's money complete with the interest right now. Otherwise your stall will be emptied of livestock, in accordance with the agreement."

"Well now, Mukhiya *ba*," Dhané said desperately, "I haven't refused to pay. But what can I do if I am unable to pay? Please just give me two months' grace. Once the buffalo has borne her calf I'll pay back the money even if I have to beg and search for it."

"What's this you're telling me now? There's an agreement between you and Baidar Saheb in this regard, in this regard, and now here he is before you. You will have to persuade him. If he agrees, there's no matter we can't come to an agreement on."

"No, no, Mukhiya Saheb, by Hariram!" the baidar protested. "Why are you chewing it over like this? When I'm losing out, there should be a proper judgment! Hariram, how long is it since he took the buffalo home? The loan was agreed for a six-month term, but now it's the fourth day of Phagun, which means that soon it will have been a whole year. He hasn't paid Hariram's interest off properly, nor does he send his people to work for me when he should. Now what more can I say as I look at his face? Hariram's agreement is right here in front of the council. You must get my money paid back to me today! If you don't, I'll take the animals from his stall."

Up until this point Dobaté Sahinla had been sitting there with his legs crossed, listening to the conversation.[50] When he heard what the baidar said, he raised himself up onto his haunches and addressed his words to Dhané's gloomy face. "I think you should pay attention. Baidar ba has much to say, and all of it is right. How is it if you take from the moneylender and then don't behave properly? Even if he can't pay back the loan, Jetha should pay the interest on it. If one debtor behaves like this, how can the rest of us approach the moneylender for a loan when we need to? If one behaves like this, won't the way be closed to others?"

Dhané was fuming, but he understood the position he was in, and he spoke humbly. "If you consider that this could also happen to you tomorrow you wouldn't talk down to me like that, Sahinla dai. But when a deer is running downhill even a calf will chase it . . . " His throat was choked with misery and anger.

Dobaté Sahinla was poor himself and indebted to several moneylenders. But he took the greatest pleasure in getting together with the rich men and tormenting neighbors who were poor like him—neighbors who worked every day, whether they were happy or sad. He wasn't alone in this either. Perhaps that's the nature of humankind: people always try to look at things from their own point of view, not from others'. If something bad happens to a man, he weeps and wails and tries to gain others' sympathy. If no one shows him any sympathy, he grows angry. But if something bad happens to someone else, he takes a kind of pleasure in it, although he makes a display of his sympathy. With one voice, the council judged in the baidar's favor and authorized him to take away Dhané's oxen and buffalo. The news that Dhané had failed to pay the baidar his money and that the council had authorized the baidar to confiscate Dhané's livestock spread quickly to every house in the village. People came from up hill and down dale to watch the show of Dhané being dispossessed. From their faces it was clear that they all had the deepest sympathy for Dhané, but they were still waiting keenly for the moment when his oxen and buffalo were untethered and led away. Perhaps if this had been canceled they would all have been disappointed. Perhaps they would have felt that they had been deprived of an entertaining spectacle.

At last the moment arrived for the baidar to remove the tethers from the animals' necks, and after this had been done two of his herdsmen drove them forward. Unable to hold back her tears, Maina ran into the house. Dhané thought of falling at the baidar's feet and grasping his legs to beg for a few days' grace, but the Dhané who was proud prevailed over the Dhané who was poor. His self-respect could not submit to his poverty. So he just stood there in silence.

13 ◇

Dhané sat beside the fire he had lit beside his vegetable patch, lost in who knows what thoughts. His son sat there, too, but when the smoke billowed up from the fresh maize stalks on the fire and got into his eyes he began to cry. The sound interrupted Dhané's train of thought.

"What happened, child? Is it the smoke? Wait just a minute! I'll chase this damned smoke away!" Dhané threw some soy pods into the fire and began to blow on it. The fire flared up, and he moved his son a little farther away. For a second he looked pensively at his son's vest, which was torn at both shoulders. He had not noticed that before now. He felt angry with Maina. "Why didn't she tell me about his vest? She could have mended it herself, it's only torn in two places. How stupid she is!" He decided that today he would use the rupee he had with him to buy two feet of homespun and get a new vest made for his son.

Maina appeared beside Dhané, carrying a bowl of maize, soybeans, and mustard seeds, which she set before him. "Look at the state of the boy's vest in this cold wind, and I have to point out to you that it's torn!" Dhané looked up and saw that Maina's blouse was in a far worse condition. Their eyes met, and then two miserable people understood each other's feelings. Maina put on a more cheerful expression and said, "I'll mend it right now. Come, *babu*, let's go inside."

She headed for the house, taking her son with her. Dhané began to pick up the maize and count the kernels as if he were finding it difficult to put them into his mouth, just like a person who is going to bathe in the Ganges in Magh and has reached its banks but finds it hard to enter the water.[51] He was sitting disconsolately over his first fistful of maize when Moté Karki came up behind him and coughed.

"Hey, daju, you'll burn right up! Dozing off there beside the fire, were you?" Karki sat down beside him.

Dhané looked up at Karki. "Where are you going so early in the morning? And have you gone blind? You've put your hat on inside out!"

"What, inside out, is it? That's what my corpse clothes are like, yes, they look exactly the same whether they're inside out or not!" Karki turned his hat right side out.

"There now, have some maize. I was having trouble finishing it, and now you've arrived, so that's good." Dhané pushed the bowl toward Karki.

"Oh, so I've turned up to help you out with the maize! Who roasted it? Bhaujyu, I suppose?"[52] Karki threw some soybean husks on the fire and warmed his hands over the flames.

"Yes, of course she did. Who else in this village would come and roast maize for us?"

"Oh, in that case I'll certainly have some. The sweetest food comes from Bhaujyu's hands!" Karki picked out some maize and chewed it. For a moment they both sat and ate in silence, then Karki asked, "Tell me, how are things these days?"

"Well, how might they be, Jetha?" Dhané heaved a long sigh. "The Sahu[53] took away my plowing oxen. Last year I stupidly went groveling to the baidar, and now I've lost the only oxen I had. This year my little patch of land is going to have to stay fallow. I don't know whether we'll get by on what I can borrow from others."

"That serf wouldn't let you keep your oxen? He's a real house-breaker, that baidar! But what's done is done. Now you should buy a plow, even if you have to borrow the money to buy it."

"Who's going to trust me enough to lend me money now? Before, I had oxen, and so they would lend money to me with them as security. Now I can only borrow if I pledge this house as security. And if I borrow, I don't know what I can repay the loan with. My own fields aren't enough even to feed us. What would I use to pay off the interest, never mind the main debt? If I could rent some fields it might be possible, but the land owners can't stand the sight of me, so who would rent me their fields?"

"Ay, now that you mention rented fields I have just re-membered that Luintel said he was giving up those fields of Nandé's this year."

"Giving them up? But those are really lovely fields, you know, and the rent is low!"

"He says he will, and why wouldn't he? He can't even cope with his own fields. Last year he was blind with greed. He has so much land already, but he's so greedy he rented more. He couldn't even get the harvesting done properly."

"Well, even if he does give them up, what good is that to me without oxen to plow them? And why would Nandé give them to me?"

"Oh, you obviously don't know Nandé. If he felt like it, he wouldn't be slow to throw down the money for a pair of oxen as well."

"Would he really? Or perhaps, if you have some money, you could help me out instead, Jetha. Should I sign the house over to you?"

"Chi! How untrusting you are, daju! If I did have any money, would I just have stood by as you suffered? You know how it is with me. If I lent you money, I would not need to worry about whether or not it came back to me. But all my money is loaned already, what can I do?"

"So speak to Nandé, would you? If you tell him, he'll believe you, no matter what. I must rent his fields from him, and I hope he'll put up the money for the oxen, too."

"Nandé dai is like this: I'll speak to his wife first; she always listens to me. If I tell her to speak to Nandé, he never refuses her anything."

"Right, Jetha, do it however you like. Otherwise, oh God, these children of mine will be lost!"

"Oh, don't worry. I'll get around the old woman, no matter what. You just make arrangements to go down to the valley to plant your seeds as soon as Baisakh arrives.[54] Getting the fields and the oxen will be my responsibility." Karki got up and stretched himself. "Right, I'm off. I'll come again after I have spoken with her."

"That's fine. And I have to set up feeding posts for the goats. If I cut them fodder, they eat it all up right there; if I let them out, there's no one to tend them." Dhané went down the hill. Karki went inside Dhané's house, calling "Bhaujyu, how are things with you?"

14 ◇

Up above, a great garland of mountains is spread out across the skyline. At its feet there lies a broad expanse of level land. Lights flicker like fireflies from the little huts on the mountainsides. The tall grasses and the boughs of the *chilaune* trees that grow on some low hills to the left of the mountains bow down, as if to welcome those who dwell below. At the edge of these hills there is a broad open meadow filled with thatch grass. Amid the grass there are a few tall pines, some *bhorla* creepers, and some huge chilaune trees.[55] This meadow is a grazing ground for the livestock that is brought down from the high pastures in winter to manure the fields.

At the edge of the meadow, the grass has been cut back, and four huts have been built; they stand in silence, each about half a furlong from the next. Seen from these huts, the water-filled rice fields in the distance look like white rocks in the moonlight. Three of the huts have walls made from branches and leaves and roofs of bamboo matting. When it is time to sow the seeds in Baisakh the farmers carry matting, cane ropes, and bamboo beams down to the valley. They cut branches, leaves, poles, and thatch from the nearby forest and build huts where they can stay while they are planting the seeds. After threshing time in Mangsir,[56] when the grain is being carried away, the huts are demolished, and the farmers return to their homes, taking the bamboo matting with them.

Only one of the huts is a permanent structure. It is longer than the others, and it has walls of wooden planking and a roof of thatch. Inside, it is divided into three separate rooms. One, on the outer side, is used as a kitchen. There is a cooking hearth to one side of the room, and along with the ordinary pots and pans of brass and bronze there is also a very large copper pitcher and two fifteen-*mana* wooden milk containers. A large butter churn and churning stick stand beside them. In the middle of the central room there is a fireplace, and around it earthen platforms have been built up to serve as beds. A straw mat is spread out on each of these for the hired laborers to sleep on. Nandé Dhakal the Sahu or his family sleep in the third room when they come to inspect the fields. In this room there are two piles of blankets.

Next to the hut there is a long cow pen. Its sides and roof are both made of bamboo matting. This hut is closed off at one end by the field boundary and open at the other. Here is a tethered buffalo that is milked for the Sahu, a pair of plowing oxen, and the Sahu's horse.

A moonlit night in the middle of Jeth.[57] The moon's light filters faintly through some thin clouds. The door of the hut is made of leafy boughs; it opens, and a wisp of smoke drifts out and disappears. Then, with a two-foot staff in one hand and a stub of tobacco wrapped in a bhorla leaf in the other, Dhané Basnet comes outside, coughs, and walks away.

15 ◇◇◇◇◇◇◇◇◇◇◇◇◇◇◇◇◇◇◇◇◇◇◇◇

Nandé Dhakal was very irritated when Luintel gave up tilling his fields. Nowadays, hardly anyone was willing to cultivate fields on a crop-sharing rental basis. Anyone who did come forward was invariably a vagabond with neither oxen to plow it nor food to eat. And so far, no one at all had come to ask him for the fields. Nandé was afraid that no crop would be grown on them this year. Then Luintel would be able to laugh. "I gave them up," he would mock. "And then who would come to plant a crop in Nandé's fields? Look, they're lying fallow!" Even if it meant buying a pair of oxen, Nandé was willing to let the fields to someone else in order to strike a blow to Luintel's pride.

One day, Nandé was pouring out his anger at Luintel to his wife. "Those fields produced so much rice the serf didn't know what to do with it all! He said he would plant them, and I rented them to him instead of to others who were planting their fields. I rented them to him, and the serf gave them up after a year! He's crazy!"

This singing of Luintel's praises might have gone on for much longer if Karki had not appeared in the doorway. After he had come in and they had talked a little about this and that, the old man went out onto the roof. Karki spoke humbly to the old woman and steered the conversation smoothly toward his suggestion that Dhané might be given the fields. The old woman told Karki to wait a minute and went up to speak to Nandé. Very soon she came back down the ladder and told Karki to fetch Dhané.

Soon, Karki and Dhané came face to face with Nandé. Nandé agreed to give Dhané the fields and was also willing to lend him the money to buy oxen and meet household expenses, with Dhané's house and land pledged as security on the loan. Once they had agreed that the fields would be cultivated that year and had signed the agreement, Dhané bade Nandé farewell and came outside with Karki. His feelings were a mixture of joy and dismay—joy at getting the fields and the money, too, and dismay at having to pledge his house and land. Now that he had obtained some fields, Dhané, like the other farmers, built a hut down in the valley and lived there most of the time after the seed had been bought and sown. Now the time had come for him to begin to transplant the seedlings into the fields. This he would start to do the very next day, and tonight there was no sleep in his eyes. Tomorrow Maina and Jhuma would come to help with the planting. But if the fields were not filled with water tonight there would be no planting tomorrow. There were many big fields there, but they were served by only two irrigation channels that came down from the hills above.

Everyone is busily planting their fields. They don't let the water into each other's fields even for a second: someone else comes and closes it off immediately, and there are constant battles over the channels. Today it is Dhané's turn to divert the water into his fields, but if he does not stand over the channel someone else takes advantage, and so Dhané has to keep going back. He went to look a little while ago and then went back to rest a while in his hut; now he is on his way out again. He is worried that, if someone shuts off the water tonight, tomorrow the soil will be dry and the fields will not be planted. And if they are not planted tomorrow he will have to wait for a week before it is his turn for the water again.[58]

16 ◇

Dhané was walking toward his fields from the far side of the valley, expecting to hear the sound of water running down the channel in the distance, but he was surprised that even as he reached the edge of the fields he could hear no sound at all. At the irrigation ditch, he stopped: there was no water in it. Only two of the terraces had filled, and a third was barely damp. "Who has shut off the water?" he thought and continued down the side of the channel. A little way off, the channel branched off into Nandé's fields. Dhané saw that the water going to his own fields had been shut off and turned into those fields instead. He looked all around carefully, and a little way off in the pale moonlight he saw a person dozing, squatting down under a homespun cloak. He crept up from behind and reached the person's side without his knowing. Dhané took a good look: it was Sané Gharti, the Sahu's plowman.[59] When Dhané gently tugged Sané's cloak, he jumped up in a fright to see Dhané standing behind him.

"You know I'm planting tomorrow, so why did you shut off my water, eh?" Dhané said in a threatening tone of voice.

"Is there any need to waste water on that useless radish patch in the marsh? The Sahu's fields have had no water since they were first planted."

"Do the marshy fields need water, you ask? Didn't you know, you serf? Didn't you know it was my turn today? When your turn comes you will probably irrigate your fields all night."

"What do you mean, 'turn'? This is all borrowed from the Sahu: the fields, the ditches. Other people only get a turn after the Sahu's fields are full."

"Will you go and talk like this when it's time for me to pay him his share of the crop? This serf lives on the Sahu's scraps, and he talks high and mighty like this!"

"Don't call me 'serf'! I don't owe you my living! Do you think I'll act on your orders? I came to divert the water on the orders of the Sahu's son."

"What name should I give to a sponger, then? We'll see how your Sahu's son is going to collect my rent this time!"

"Until you got the fields you waggled your head all meekly in front of the Sahu, like a dog wagging its tail. 'Give me the fields,' you said. 'Buy me some oxen,' you said. But now you start speaking rudely about that same Sahu's son. They'll just take your fields away, so don't shoot your mouth off!"

Dhané could not put up with this. By nature he was not a person who put up with other people's taunts very well. So he gave Sané Gharti a slap on the face.

"That's for you, serf! Do you think a sponger like you can say whatever he likes to me?" Dhané landed a couple more blows on his back. Sané Gharti was still young, and he was no match for Dhané. Dhané's hard blows made him whimper.

"You think I'm not your equal, don't you! But watch out, you'll find out in the end when the Sahu's son strips you of all your pride! You humbled yourself and laid your hat at his feet, and just because you got some fields in the end your success has gone to your head and your feet aren't on the ground! If he doesn't take the fields back tomorrow, I am not my father's son!"

Off he went back to his hut, muttering all sorts of things as he went. "Go on then, go and tell your tales, drag out whatever you can!" Dhané told him, as he reached the channel and turned the water into his own fields. Once it had filled up the first terrace, he used a stick to make dents in two or three places on the terrace rims so that the water would flow down to the other terraces. Then he went up and washed the mud from his arms and legs. The moon was sinking in the west as he returned wearily to his hut.

Nandé Dhakal's youngest son had just returned home, having completed his government office examinations. From an early age he had had a tyrannical nature, and he had been brought up with great indulgence, so that once he came home there was always some quarrel or other going on in the village. He would assemble a gang of youths, usually plowmen or servants from his home, and visit the village at night. There he would steal a goat from someone's pen, or beat up a village lad, or harass one of the girls. He was happy when he made other people miserable, and it was his nature to tease and humiliate those who were weaker or poorer than himself. The villagers cursed him behind his back, but they could not say anything to his face because he was the Sahu's son. Nandé had noticed his son getting into bad habits and had sent him down to the valley on the pretext that his son could look after his affairs there. So these days the son lived in the valley, and his principal tasks were walking around the field terraces killing doves with a catapult, riding into the nearby forest on horseback and hunting with a loaded gun, and so on. He had spent this day chasing doves around the fields and had returned to the hut in the evening. It was he who had ordered Sané Gharti to divert the water into the fields that night and to guard the channel.

As the night entered its second quarter, the Sahu's son had already finished one nap and was beginning to doze again. Sané Gharti came sniveling into the hut. His sobs woke the young

Sahu, who scolded him. "Oh, what's happened to this stupid corpse now? Why is he crying, has someone beaten him up, or what is it?"

The question made Sané snivel all the more. "Dhané Basnet didn't just dishonor me, he beat me, too. And he called the Sahus all sorts of rude names. He dammed the channel to our fields and left no water for us at all. He shut all the water off and made it flow into his own fields."

The young Sahu's ears burned when he heard this. "Who does that serf think he is? Doesn't he know who I am?" For a moment he ground his teeth angrily in silence. Perhaps he was wondering what he might do to take his revenge. Then he told Sané, "First thing in the morning, take a buffalo to that serf's seedbed and let it loose. Then how will he plant his fields?"

◈ ◈ ◈

Dhané set out for the fields with his hoe in the early morning light. His plan was to prepare the four or five terraces on the marshier side where the oxen could not work and to have the job done before the women arrived from home to begin the planting. As he arrived at the top of the fields the expression of joy, vigor, and eagerness that had been on his face changed to a look of despair, remorse, and frustration. His eyes moved over the seedbed, where the Sahu's buffalo was grazing happily on his six-inch seedlings, with Sané Gharti sitting to one side enjoying the show. Dhané's misery and fury turned him into a madman. He was shocked to see the wheel of his fortune cheating him time after time. He had dreamed up such a future for himself on the basis of these fields, he had poured out his labor on these fields with such joy, but now . . .

Unable to control himself any longer, he raised his hoe in both hands with the blade turned upward and charged at the buffalo like a lunatic. The ground was wet, so the buffalo's hooves had sunk into the mud, and it could not move quickly. Dhané caught up with it and dealt it six or seven blows with the back of his hoe: in his anger and pain, he had even forgotten his fondness for animals. Not until a few moments later did he feel regret and realize that his attack had been futile because the buffalo was not at fault. The buffalo reached the far side of the field and lay down on the slope. Sané Gharti ran in terror to the hut to inform his master. "*Lau!*" he yelled. "Basnet's killed the pregnant buffalo!"

◈ **18**

Soon after Sané had gone, Dhané's anger and excitement subsided, and fear and dread took their place. "If the Sahu's pregnant buffalo has come to any harm at all, we'll be wiped out of the village. Very soon the whole affair is going to reach his ears, and then these fields I got with such difficulty will be taken away from me. Oh Lord, what will become of me now?"

Dhané went down to the fields, thinking about all the calamities the future held for him. He shook all over as he went to the buffalo's side and tried to raise it to its feet. But it was badly injured, and he could do nothing on his own. Hopelessly, he went back to the hut. In his mind he repeated the same prayer over and over again: "Oh Lord, do not let anything happen to the buffalo; deliver me from this crisis. In my ignorance I destroyed her; forgive me, Lord."

The Sahu's men came and managed somehow to raise the buffalo and take it away. Dhané sat inside his hut, nursing his grief. Maina arrived with their hired laborers, but when they heard about the incident the laborers realized there would be no planting that day, and they went back home. But a fire was kindled in Maina's heart. If anything happened to the buffalo as a result of the beating, what would become of her husband? She could not think beyond this. Deep in her heart she promised the goddess's temple a pair of doves so that no evil would befall her husband.

The man and the woman both sat in the hut for one whole day, sad and exhausted. Neither had the strength to raise the other's spirits. The buffalo had destroyed every seedling. And who would give them new seeds, now that the planting was in full swing? Without seeds it would be impossible to plant the fields this year. In the evening, they simply locked up their hut and went home.

A terrible sense of foreboding tormented Dhané and Maina night and day. Eventually, what they feared became reality. One evening three days after the incident, Nandé's herdsman Chimsé came to tell them that the Sahu's buffalo had died that morning. When he learned that the Sahu had decided to call a meeting of the village council, Dhané lost all hope. Before he left, Chimsé conveyed an order from Nandé and the subba: "You must present yourself before the council tomorrow."

Dhané lay on his bed with an empty heart. "What judgment will the council make tomorrow?" Maina asked miserably. He had already more or less guessed what the judgment would be. But after they had judged him, what punishment would they impose? This was the question that hounded him now. He suppressed his anxiety and got up to wipe the tears from Maina's face. "They'll make whatever judgment they make," he said. "Can worrying put off what must be?" Dhané's kindness broke Maina's self-control, and she hid her face in his lap and sobbed. Dhané stroked her hair in an attempt to console her and said, "Oh, why do you cry like this? Your husband has not died! Why worry when I am still with you? And what can really happen to us anyway? We certainly won't lose our lives: it's just that our debts will increase. One day the good times will come back, eh? Do you think I'll die without paying those serfs what I owe them?" Dhané tried to console Maina like this, then he sent her off to bed. He lay down as well, but sleep was too afraid to approach either of them.

◈ ◈ ◈

When Dhané reached Nandé's yard the next morning, a large gathering had assembled—the mukhiya, the subba, the baidar, and the good gentlemen of the council. He sat down to one side of them, and they began to consider his case. He was asked many questions, and the gentlemen exchanged opinions. Then with one voice they decided that Dhané was guilty. No one took Dhané's side, except for the mukhiya. Just so "the scales of justice are not out of balance," the mukhiya declared, "Let me say in this regard that it is not fitting to state only one side of things. Now, it is agreed that the Sahu's buffalo did eat Dhané's seedlings, and so he should repay Dhané an equivalent amount of grain. As far as the value of the buffalo is concerned, that is something that Dhané must pay back. Isn't that how it should be?"

But an elderly gentleman disagreed. "How can it be right just to do it in terms of market prices?" he said. "If we just ask him for the price of the buffalo, then again and again people will kill a pregnant buffalo and then pay to replace it, and that will be that! Dhané should pay the full penalty for killing a pregnant buffalo. These are straightforward matters!"

From a corner at the back a low voice was heard to say, "If that's so, a penalty should also be paid by the person who knowingly let a buffalo loose on someone else's seedbed in the middle of the planting. It's not a bull, this buffalo, is it?"

It is not certain that all the councilors heard these words, but Nandé immediately turned his red eyes in the direction from which the voice had come and said, "Hey, serf, be quiet! Who told you to open your mouth in the presence of these gentlemen?" And that person did not dare to speak again.

The decision was announced. Dhané was to pay 150 rupees, the value of the buffalo, plus a 75-rupee fine for killing a pregnant buffalo. He was given a warning that if he ever killed any livestock in the same way again he would be expelled from the village.

Because his buffalo had destroyed Dhané's seedlings, the Sahu was to give Dhané 15 pathi of rice.

As soon as the judgment had been announced, Nandé declared before the gentlemen of the council that Dhané could not have the fields anymore. It was decided that Dhané owed the Sahu a total of 575 rupees, because the money the Sahu had given him earlier to buy the oxen and to meet household expenses, plus interest, had to be added to the fine of 225 rupees. Because he could not pay this immediately, Dhané asked to be allowed to make a bond. So he was given two and a half months to pay, and a new agreement was drawn up. This stated that if Dhané did not pay the whole sum with interest within two and a half months the Sahu could have Dhané's house and livestock valued and raise the money from their sale. Once Dhané had affixed his mark to the agreement, the council meeting was over.

◈ 19

Today, Maina has risen after two days of fever, and she sits on a mat on the verandah stripping the kernels from some maize cobs. Her hands are busily engaged in the task, while through her mind there flows a rapid stream of thoughts. She is aghast to see crisis piling on crisis in her life. Human life is considered to be the best in all of God's creation, but she has begun to wonder

whether the lives of the poor and the sorrowful are any better than those of animals. Those who resort to oppressing, mistreating, and dishonoring the truthful honest poor live lives of pleasure in palaces of gold, but the poor who live at the very limits of exertion cannot find a way to put their hands to their mouths. Is this the script of fortune that the Creator has written out? There is no answer to any of her questions. And so to console herself she says, "Perhaps this is something we earned in a previous life."

For many days the rain has not allowed her to lay the grain out to dry in the sun. Today she has decided to put her trust in the sun, which is playing hide-and-seek among the clouds, and she takes the maize she has removed from the cobs, puts it into a basket, and takes it out to the yard to spread it on a bamboo mat. Sometimes Surya disappears behind the clouds, then after a moment he appears again,[60] and so it goes on.

Maina had just gone back to sit down on the mat and deal with the remaining maize when Thuli came down the hill.

"Has the fever gone, Bhaujyu?" Thuli asked.

"Yes, for the time being it has, but perhaps it will be back this evening. What trust can you put in this corpse of a fever! Sit down now, child, where are you off to?"

"Nowhere at all. I have been sleeping and sleeping, and now I have come down here. I was going to weed the maize, but the field is muddy, so I just gave up for the time being. It's been raining so much these past few days it's hardly let me open my eyes." Thuli sat down on the mat.

"That's right, child, this rain has finished us off, hasn't it! I expect Kanchi has gone to Sahinla Gharti's place, thinking it might be sunny today. Did she say she was hoeing their maize?"[61]

"Oh really? Is Kanchi Didi doing exchange labor at Gharti's place today?"[62]

"Yes, I think it was her turn the day before yesterday, but the rain kept her in." The conversation paused for a moment. Both women began to pick off maize kernels. After a while Thuli said hesitantly, "Bhaujyu, I've been meaning to ask you something for days, but various jobs keep getting in the way and making me forget."

"What is it, then? Ask away!" Maina glanced at Thuli.

"Should I ask you, I wonder? Will you be angry?"

"Oh no, do come on now, mori, would I get angry with you simply for asking a question? Don't chew on it, tell me what it is." Maina tried to laugh.

"Well, Bhaujyu, I don't know why, but nowadays Kanchi Didi looks different to me. She doesn't talk very much, and she walks around looking sad." Thuli paused in her work.

"Well, I don't know either. Perhaps she isn't feeling well. She doesn't tell us much."

"I am worried, Bhaujyu." Thuli became grave.

"What are you worried about, what do you mean, mori?" Maina was alarmed, and she looked quizzically at Thuli.

"Bhaujyu, you are so simple. You are with her night and day, so how can you not understand even a little? Very soon the whole village will find out."

"Stop embroidering it with flowers, just tell me straight, what is the matter?" The color had drained from Maina's face.

"Well, I believe that Jhuma is pregnant. Have you no inkling of this?"

Maina looked as if she had fallen off a roof. Now she understood what had been puzzling her: why Jhuma had lost her taste for spicy food, why her gait was less sprightly than before. And she remembered that once Jhuma had mentioned that her monthly *dharma* had stopped. But at the time Maina had just assumed that it was late and had paid no further attention to it. She had not had the faintest idea.

In despair, Maina asked, "Who has she been going around with, Nani, do you know? You are her friend after all, whatever might happen."

"Well, who knows? For a few days I thought she was going around with a stranger, but that was a long time ago. When she comes home this evening you will have to ask her properly. If you ask her about it while there is still time, some solution will turn up."

"I'll have to ask her," Maina said briefly.

Soon after that Thuli left. Maina was at her wits' end. She decided that she would think about it a lot, and then when Jhuma came home in the evening they would make the right decisions. She stood up and saw that the sky was full of clouds. She was afraid that the cold wind would dampen the grain, so she began to pick it all up again.

20 ◇

At this point it would be best for us to go back to an incident that occurred some months earlier. After they parted company by the swing at Dasain, Jhuma and the soldier did not meet again for months. It is not possible to say whether the soldier thought about Jhuma, but each day Jhuma's heart sought him out at least once. For the first month Jhuma was very distraught that she had not seen him again, but even this kind of distress lessens with the passing of time. In her heart there remained only a small remnant of her memory of him.

One day in the middle of Magh, Jhuma had gone into the forest to cut some fodder. All around her there were bare rugged mountains that made her feel alone and cut off, and there was no greenness anywhere. The whole of nature had dried up. All through the forest the fallen leaves lay dry and withered. Even the steep tumbling stream had dried up, and its melancholy sound came from deep down below. Here and there white flowers bloomed, peaceful like oases in a desert. Beside the stream two sheaves of foliage grew from a *gagun* bush, and Jhuma gathered them up. By the time she had cut another bundle of thatch grass, she felt melancholy, too.

She sat down on a flat rock and rested for a while. She did not enjoy seeing nature all around her so lacking in beauty. She began to remember many things from the past, and then she recalled the soldier. "He hasn't visited for many days. Might he have forgotten me? He won't be as loving as I am, will he now! But then, why shouldn't he be? Poor thing, he spoke of marriage that day, and he must be upset now because I seemed unwilling."

A flood of emotion had washed her far away, and to push it back again she sang a song that echoed through the forest:

ukali jyanko cipleto dhungo
dui jiu naran basaunla
bandhana maya thyammai.
yo man jasto tyo man bhae
mayako dhago ni kasaaunla
bandhana maya thyammai.

On a flat rock on the steep hill of life
Our two bodies, Lord, will sit.
Pledge your love forever.
If his heart feels the same as mine
We will tie the thread of love.
Pledge your love forever.

She had just finished her song and was thinking of going down the hillside to cut two more bundles of foliage when someone suddenly spoke behind her.

"Hello, Jhuma, have you come to cut fodder?"

"*Aabui*, it's you!⁶³ What are you doing in the forest?" The words sprang from her mouth, filled with joy and delight.

"I was on my way up the hill by the main path up there. Your voice drew me here." The soldier sat down beside her.

"I thought you might have forgotten me." Jhuma lowered her head as she spoke.

"I think about you night and day. . . . If only you felt the same!"

"And how do you know that I don't? How do you know my feelings aren't even stronger than yours?"

"Is that the truth then?" The soldier took hold of her hand.

"Chi! If someone saw us, what would they say?" Jhuma pulled her hand away.

"Oh, who would be watching us out here in the forest? Have you gathered enough fodder yet?"

"I was going to stop when I'd made three bundles. I'd carry on cutting if there were enough foliage."

"Do the animals eat *dudilo*?"[64]

"Yes, but where can they get it? They'd love it if I could get some for them!"

"I'll climb up that tree. You collect it down here, all right?"

"Aabui! Can men who've been in the army climb trees as well?" Jhuma was surprised and amused.

"Oh! We've been trained to do everything!"

The soldier went up to the dudilo tree, and Jhuma followed him. By the time he had finished throwing down the foliage and had climbed down again, Jhuma had collected it into sheaves and was bundling them together. The soldier stood nearby and looked all around him. After a few moments Jhuma came back and sat down on the rock. He sat down right beside her, and said very gently, "Jhuma, will you come to Mugalan? I am going in Asar."[65]

"Well, I was all ready to go before, you know, but how could I leave just like that?"

"I will take you with me for sure. Whatever happens, I won't forget." He was holding Jhuma's left hand in both of his. She tried to pull it away, but he tightened his grip.

"You're mine, Jhuma, no one can take you away from me."

Jhuma was trapped in his arms. Although it was a winter's day, there were beads of sweat on her face. A desperate look came onto her face. She struggled for a long time to free herself, but then her body became limp, and after a moment everything was ruined.

The soldier told Jhuma that he would be busy in the office until Asar but assured her that after that he would take her to Mugalan. Then he went on his way.

Jhuma stood up. Her heart was heavy, and it burned with remorse. Today she had been forced to give up the virginity that keeps young girls secure in their status, and now even it regarded her with contempt. Until this day she had had the courage to face society without fear, but now she felt that she had fallen very low. She picked up the load of fodder and set out for home, tying the soldier's promise into a firm knot in the headscarf of her trust. What else could she have done, after all?

21 ◈

When she returned home from Sahinla Gharti's, evening had already fallen. Across the ravine the cicadas were singing their evening *arati*.[66] Jhuma entered the grounds of the house, picked some leeches off her body and tossed them aside, and then washed her hands and feet and went inside.

The two women finished washing the pots and went to the mill. Jhuma began to turn the millstone single-mindedly. Today Jhuma was very different. She had always been very lively and very keen to sing sangini songs as they milled. She had chattered away to her Bhaujyu. But now she was taciturn. Regret was stamped deeply on her face, and she was immersed in a secret worry. Her body was showing signs that were making her very anxious, but she could not accept that what she feared was true. Her heart trembled, and she abandoned the train of thought that led in that direction. Was it true, or was it not? She had been denying it to herself right up until today, when Maina's question— "Are you pregnant? Tell me the truth, what is the matter?"— woke her as if from a dream. Thoughts began to course through her brain once more. Gently, Maina pressed her for the truth, and Jhuma told her everything. She told her of her first encounter with the soldier, of how he had stayed in their house that night, of their later meetings at the weekly market and at the swing, and in the end about the incident in the forest. She also said that the soldier was going to take her to Mugalan in Asar and that she had complete trust in him. When she heard these words from the mouth of such an innocent girl, Maina was aghast and made plain her anger at Jhuma's foolishness. Then she wept for a long time in despair at the log that fate had flung at them.

◇ 22

Early next morning, Maina burned incense and offered water to the sun, but her mind was not on these tasks, and she was filled with impatience. Dhané had gone out somewhere at dawn. Maina sent for Thuli, and soon the two of them were sitting talking in the storehouse. Maina told Thuli all about Jhuma and said, "Child, you have a friend[67] at Limbugaon, don't you? You have an excuse for going there. That man's house is there, too, she tells me. Go and confirm this, then come back and tell me. That corpse has really done his worst!"

"Yes, of course. I will go today. I'll stay with my friend there tonight, and I'll let you know before your morning meal tomorrow."

"Child, please do take the trouble. It would be best to get that corpse committed to marrying her and make him shoulder his responsibility."

"Oh, Bhaujyu, it's become such a worry for you!"

"What else can I do, child? If her brother discovers this, he'll throw her out! When I look at her face, I do love her so." The tears slipped from Maina's eyes.

"Bhaujyu, it's late. I'll go and get ready to leave." Thuli walked back up the hill.

The next day, when it was time to let the livestock out, Dhané ate some millet gruel and then took the oxen out to graze. Although Maina called her repeatedly, Jhuma would not come to eat, claiming that she was unwell. Nor did she go out to work that day. She sat in the vegetable garden with her eyes fixed on the lane, looking out for Thuli. She waited fearfully for the news that Thuli would bring, wondering what it would mean for her. A lot of time went by, and thoughts began to play in Jhuma's mind.

"Why is she late? This is just like Thuli! Wherever she goes, she never comes back when she says she will. She will be chattering away to her friend, or perhaps she couldn't find the soldier. Did he lie to me when he told me he lived at Limbugaon? Has he already gone to Mugalan? But no, he wouldn't deceive me, he was not that sort. Why would he leave without me?"

Jhuma tired of the long wait. She was just making her way inside when she heard Thuli panting in the lane below and saw her coming slowly along, sweating profusely. Anxiously, she went down to the alley to meet her.

"Aabui! How late you are, Thuli! I was looking out for you for so long my eyes are sore!" Jhuma embraced her.

"What could I do? I wanted to be quick, but it took longer than I thought." Thuli wore a gloomy expression. "You'll hear whatever I have to tell you soon enough, why are you so anxious?"

Jhuma was alarmed to see Thuli looking so grave. The two of them reached the garden, and Thuli made as if to enter the house, but Jhuma caught hold of her hand and drew her aside.

"Where are you going? Tell me right now—what happened?" Jhuma made her sit down.

"Where is Bhaujyu?" Thuli asked.

"Leave Bhaujyu out of it, tell me first! What happened?"

"What can I tell you, sister? How can I tell you?"

"What do you think I am? Do you think I am afraid? Whatever happened, just tell me about it and don't hide anything. I can bear it." Jhuma braced herself.

"It's a complete disaster. You did what you did, and you trusted such a corpse of a man you didn't even know. They say he left in Phagun." The words came mechanically from Thuli's mouth.

For a moment Jhuma could see nothing. Then it was as if she was seeing everything only dimly in the distance: the big rock in the vegetable garden, the alleyway, Thuli, and everything else. In her ears there rang the sound of many faraway voices. After a long while she heard Thuli call her name, and it was only then that she jumped and said "Yes?" Everything seemed like a dream to her. Thuli linked her left arm with Jhuma's right and asked, "Kanchi Didi, what should I say to Bhaujyu?"

As if resigned, and only half-conscious, Jhuma replied, "Tell her the truth, Thuli. It's not something we can hide. We'll have to tell her in the end anyway."

23 ◇

Thuli went indoors, but Jhuma remained sitting in the garden. When she heard from Thuli that the soldier had left in Phagun, Maina was beside herself. She could not tell whether she had been buried beneath the earth or was still above it.

Maina was only seven years older than Jhuma, but she was not merely Jhuma's sister-in-law; she was her mother, too. When Maina first stepped into this house, Jhuma had been a small motherless girl. It was Maina who had brought her up, who had reared her. Jhuma had learned everything from her. Although she had been parted from her mother when she was small, Jhuma had not been deprived of a mother's love.

There is no mother who is not distraught when she considers a daughter's sad plight. For a devoted, simple-hearted woman like Maina, the crisis that had arisen in Jhuma's life, the calumny that would now be heaped on her husband, and the stain that would now mark a family that had never bowed to anything before were not petty matters. Perhaps she would have been less worried by the prospect of everything they owned being taken away from them than by the threat of damage being done to the unblemished honor of their line.

Injury is the root cause of anger. The blow that Maina's heart had suffered made her angry, and she decided that Jhuma was responsible for this whole affair, that Jhuma carried all the blame. This was not wholly true, of course, but there were enough facts to support it. In the simple course of events, Jhuma was innocent, but when one approached the secret that lay behind it, it was impossible to say that she was entirely guiltless.

Jhuma's simplicity and weakness had enabled the soldier to commit his crime. When women want something, they do not try to assess it critically. They run along a ravine of certain belief without looking either up or down, and they have no inkling of the pit that lies in wait for them. At this stage they do not have brains; their hearts are like machines that simply want to take and possess.

Unable to restrain herself, Maina went outside and began to hurl abuse at Jhuma. The fire in her heart came out of her mouth in flames: "What will happen when your brother finds out? You've rubbed soot in all our faces, where can we hide them now? Tomorrow, when word gets out, all the villagers will spit on you, and then where will you hide? It would be better for you to die before that happens; now you have no choice but to die. . . ."

Maina went on shouting like this without pause, and she shed a flood of tears, but Jhuma paid no attention to anything else she said. That single phrase had lodged itself in her brain: "Now you have no choice but to die."

All that day it went round and round in her head. She thought to herself that there really was no alternative for her. She had been terribly misled. Tomorrow the news would spread through the whole village. Then the friends who once embraced her would abhor her. Voices would surround her, saying "Sinner! Sinner!" If Maina, who had loved her like a daughter until yesterday, could wish her dead, how would others behave? Could she endure all that? And she remembered the soldier and the love she had declared to him, and her heart asked her a question: "Was that love?" The answer came back: "No, that was merely youthful impulsiveness. It was just a momentary pleasure." Her faith in the soldier shattered like a mirror, and hatred took its place. Today she realized that her soul had been sullied, and she hated herself. Again and again her own heart told her, "You deserve to be punished. You are a sinner."

"And what will be the penance for this?" she wondered. Then she remembered what Maina had said: "Now you have no choice but to die."

24 ◇

Only the first quarter of the night had passed, but the whole village was already silent. It was the rainy season, the season of labor for those who depend on the fields. All day they are constantly busy, each with his own tasks. The four quarters of the night are the time for them to rest. Wearied by their days of work, they eat, drink, and lie down, and then they go to travel abroad in the heavenly realm of the goddess of sleep.

Every living being in the village is wrapped in the pleasurable embrace that nature provides, but there is no sleep in the eyes of one of the flowers of human society. Her soul wrestles with remorse and the admonitions of her conscience.

Haay, conscience! You are the grandeur of human society. Only with you can the standard of human society be raised. You are the herder who guides humanity along, but there is no real joy in being driven by you. Or let us say that you are not used for satisfaction or for peace. You deride the past and then tear it into shreds that you scorch in the fire of regret. You point to the future and constantly make us afraid. And you are always busy unearthing the mistakes of the present. You spread wings of hope and aspiration, and you send educated people flying in search of a happiness that continually moves away. But who has ever met with peace and joy?

A dark night, and darker still because clouds have filled the sky and covered the stars. The whole of nature wears a black cloak. The darkness and the silence make this night a frightening one.

Then the main door of a small house opened and slowly closed. A white figure[68] came out into the yard and could be seen making its way quickly toward the main path. The path forked at Bagedanda. The lower fork went to the next village; the higher led to the forest. The figure paused where the path forked and turned to look back. Then it left the lower path and went quickly along the path that led to the forest. A fierce wind parted the clouds a little, and a few stars appeared. After walking for a while along the path, which cut through the middle of the jungle like a white line drawn across a slate, the figure left the path and headed for the fields. Taking to the field ridges, it crossed the fields and arrived at the Ragé cliff, where it stopped still.

Ragé cliff was the name given to a rocky precipice that must be thousands of feet high—looking down from its summit made you giddy. Many cows, oxen, and people had fallen from it and liberated themselves from the world. At its foot, many souls had freed themselves from the bonds of life and taken rest. The old folk said that an Old Woman of the Forest lived on these cliffs. They said that sometimes on new moon nights she would put on white clothes and come out onto the hillside at midnight to dance, making the bells on her anklets jingle. But no one who had ever set out to look for her had ever come forward to claim a sighting. Once, several of the young dhami boys of the village had gone there on a new moon night to watch the Old Woman dance and had waited all night but seen nothing. Instead, whether it was by chance, because they had missed a night's sleep, or because they had been chilled by the dew, several of them became ill afterward. Then the story spread through the village that the Old Woman had found them. Because of this, the herders did not often go that way, even in the daytime, for fear of the Old Woman.

The figure looks down from the edge of the cliff and thinks, "Before I was born, they say, an ox named Ragé fell and found rest at the foot of this cliff. That is why everyone calls it the Ragé cliff." And today this figure, too, is weary: it wants to sleep at the foot of the cliff, never to wake again. It needs a long rest. It no longer has any strength left to bear the slaps and blows of society. No longer can it struggle against a society that just looks on as it is beaten and weeps. Breaking its stream of thoughts in midflow, it rises and goes to stand at the edge of the cliff. It looks once at the sky and says who knows what. Then, just as it closes its eyes tightly and is about to throw itself down, a pair of strong arms grips it firmly.

When Maina came downstairs early that morning, tears were streaming from her eyes. Sobbing with fright, she went to Dhané's side. Dhané was already awake, but he lay there with his head on his hand, his elbow resting on his chaff-filled pillow. Somewhat surprised, he asked, "Oh no, what has happened? Why are you crying so early in the morning?"

"The child is not in her bed. I thought she'd be outside, but I can't see her anywhere." Maina was overcome with worry, and her voice was choked.

"Is that something for you to cry about? What does it matter where she's gone? She'll have gone out somewhere or other. She'll come back again, won't she?"

"You don't understand. She is not herself at all. She's gone far away, I'm sure of it!"

"What is she up to, then? What's happened that she should go far away for no reason?"

"Well, what can I say? I'm just about dead with fear."

"Why? What have you discovered? Tell me!"

Fearfully, Maina told him all about Jhuma. She also told him how she had shouted at her the previous day. Once he had heard everything from Maina, Dhané was not especially surprised that Jhuma had gone missing, nor did he show any sorrow. Having suffered so many blows of fate, he had become hard in a certain sense. Now there was a stain on his family's reputation, and the world would mock them. This was certainly something of a blow,

but his greatest sorrow was that he had been unaware of his sister's condition although she lived right there in his house. Before Maina told him, he had not had the faintest idea.

A question occurred to him: "Whose fault is this? Is it Jhuma's? Yes, of course it's her fault!" But his limited intellect would not accept this. After a moment he thought, "No it's not; it's my fault! I wasn't able to get her married when I ought, and now all this has happened. If I had had the money to get her married or if you didn't need money to marry a girl off and I didn't have to fill the bellies of this whole village at a wedding feast, I would not have had to witness this day. The fault is mine. It's the fault of my poverty, of my helplessness. It's the fault of the fate that has made me poor and of the Creator who wrote my broken fate!"

"The Creator? Is it the Creator who writes our fate?" Today for some reason his small brain was pursuing arguments that were full of hidden revolutionary facts. "Why would fate be so biased? The laborers who wear out their bones in sweat cry out for flour, while those who gather up their bones to suck have other pleasures. Is this what fate really is? No, the Creator is not so unjust! Fate is made by human arrangement. Fate depends on the good order of society, on cooperation in society, on the chances and facilities you can get in society." Today, if he had had even the smallest opportunity, if his society had cared to understand his plight, would his labors not have borne fruit? If society had not been so ready to mock Jhuma's small misdemeanor, would she have left the house today in such desperation? Was the fault hers alone? Was it not the fault of the soldier, who had taken advantage of an innocent girl to gratify his desires? But it is the helpless girl and her family who are punished by society. This was the sum of Dhané's argument with his conscience. Today his heart was rebelling.

Again and again Maina wept and begged Dhané to search for Jhuma, but Dhané showed no concern. He answered her bluntly and then was silent: "If she is dead, we will hear of it. There's no need to search for her."

◇ 26

There is no need for a telegram or a radio to deliver bad news. Once something has come out it gets into the wind and flies into everyone's ears. At the morning mealtime three girls were talking at the waterfall spring.

"I hear Jhuma's walked out, is it true?" Goma asked her younger sister.

"I don't know. What do we know about other households' affairs? I have heard it said she's not there," Ghartini replied.

"Well, I've suspected this for a while, you know. From the way she behaved, I thought she was going to take to her heels. That's how it seemed to me."

"We shouldn't talk like this now. If she's gone off somewhere, she could still come back this evening. She won't stay away for long, will she?" said Ghartini.

"Oh, so she's back already, is she? And she's told you where she's been, I suppose?"

Thuli had remained quiet till then. But when she heard what they were saying she said, "I'll tell you something, but you mustn't tell anyone else, all right?"

"What is it?" asked Goma, "Oh do tell us, do!"

"First you both must swear that you'll never tell anyone, and then I'll tell you," said Thuli.

"Oh!" cried Ghartini. "How distrustful she is, this Thuli! Tell us what it is, won't you? Have we ever gone around the village talking about you so that you think we'll start gossiping now?"

"It's not a thing you should tell anyone else about. I'm only telling you two," said Thuli. "Keep it to yourselves. Anyway, Jhuma—well, she's with child! It's that soldier corpse's child, they say."

"Really?" exclaimed Goma. "Well, I had my suspicions! So has she gone off with him, then?"

"Do you think he'd stick around here?" said Thuli. "He went back to Mugalan in Phagun, they say. Where she's gone today I don't know. Yesterday her sister-in-law gave her a real telling-off, and now the poor thing's walked out."

"Eee, the poor thing! Where can she have gone in her condition?" said Ghartini. "That so-called Rikute serf really lied through his teeth, didn't he!"

The three of them went on talking as they set off home with their water jars. Before they had even finished decanting the water back home, Goma and Kanchi Ghartini had already told one or two people, saying, "Don't tell anyone, do you hear?" The people they told told several others, pledging them to silence, too. Thus talk of Jhuma traveled from the women's society to the men's. Soon the whole village was whispering.

Many of them said, "We must cut Dhané off from sharing our water; we don't know who did this or what he was. How can we share water with his household when we don't know how long this affair has been going on?" Others argued, "Oh, it's not right to raise the matter of pollution by water anymore, the Legal Code has done away with that." But some came out with a response to that: "When has it ever been right to ignore the customs that have come to us from our forefathers?"[69]

The villagers had many theories about Jhuma's disappearance. Several thought she had gone somewhere far away and committed suicide. Others said, "She and the soldier had made plans beforehand, and she's gone off with him." The various reports went around and around the village.

Maina did not stop weeping all day. She sorely regretted abusing Jhuma the day before. But Dhané was burning deep inside. His mood was clear from the expression on his face. He spent the whole day sitting at home and did not go out at all.

27

⬦ ⬦

God is everywhere. This is as true as the existence of the sun. The Lord sees everything a person does and everything that befalls him. When injustice and oppression go beyond extremes and those who suffer them need assistance, then in some shape or form, help always comes from the Lord. It was a coincidence, merely a coincidence. But who was involved in contriving such a coincidence? It was that unseen power, for sure.

On the night the disguised figure left its house and headed for the Ragé cliff, Moté Karki had by chance gone to turn water into a field near the edge. A gust of wind blew his torch out, and he squatted on the ridge of a terrace listening to the sound of the water in the irrigation ditch. His gaze fell on a white figure flowing past in the far distance. What a surprise! What was this out here in the night? Closer and closer, lau! It was coming toward him! Perhaps it was the Old Woman of the Ragé cliff! Karki was alarmed. To avoid the wrath of the Old Woman who was advancing toward him, he slowly climbed down two or three terraces and stood on a field ridge. He thought of running away, but then he felt braver, and curious, too. "I must get a close look at the Old Woman," he thought. "What can happen to me, after all? I'll only die if my days are over. And who do I have to weep for me?" He squatted down, and the figure came very close; then he began to have doubts. "But it looks like a real woman!" There were only three terraces between them, and what a surprise: it was Jhuma! What was she doing here in the middle of the night?

Jhuma approached the Ragé cliff, and Karki had no time to wonder why. He followed her without her knowing what he was doing.

When some unknown force stopped her from behind just as she was about to throw her body from the Ragé cliff, Jhuma felt as if she had woken from a dream. The senses that had already died returned to her. She turned back from the midst of her doubt and fear and saw Karki smiling before her.

"Karki daju! What are you doing here at this hour?"

"I came to turn water into the field. But why have you come here in the night?"

"Me? Tell me, why did you catch me? You should have let me die! What kind of suffering is this, that I cannot even die?" As she spoke she felt giddy, and she fell to her knees.

Karki knelt down beside her and said, "How can you die, just by deciding to die though your days are not over? You have not finished your life, have you?"

"Enough, enough! My days are over! With what face can I live now?"

"They say we only get this body by acquiring great merit, so it's wrong to throw it away like that. Kanchi Didi, take your time and tell me, what is afflicting you? What suffering makes you try to die? I will do whatever I can to help you."

"It's not worth telling, Karki! Do not listen to me, you will be touched by my sin. I am a sinner, a real sinner!"

"That is what you say, but it is not so. In my eyes you are like a goddess. Did the soldier desert you? I can easily recognize the signs."

"Do not mention that corpse; you warned me about him yourself. At that time my eyes were blind, and your advice was like poison to me. What to do? You can't get inside a person's mind."

"But what happened? Tell me a little more plainly."

"Everything you might expect when I had put my trust in him. You have understood already, why do you pretend that you have not? Is it to make me ashamed?"

"He said he would take you away, then he left without you. That is what pains you, is it not? I heard he'd gone back just the other day."

"If you knew, why didn't you tell me?"

"What did I know? I thought you already knew. Did I think you would want to die just because he didn't take you with him? And he'll be back, you know!"

"Who's going to look for him whether he comes or goes? He's gone, and he's left me here unable to show my face in front of anyone."

"Why? What has happened?"

"Don't you know? His sin is growing in my stomach. I am with child."

"Ay, so that's it, so it went that far."

"So tell me now, with what face can I live on?" Jhuma covered her face with her hand and wept.

"Don't cry, Kanchi Didi. I'll take you to him, wherever he is."

"No! I never want to see his face again! I'd rather throw myself down and die!"

"If that's so, I have only one thing to say. Come with me."

"Where? Back to our village?"

"No, far away. Somewhere where these villagers can't find you and taunt you."

"Why should you go off and suffer with a sinner like me? I cannot throw off my sin!"

"You have no sin, Kanchi Didi! The child you bear shall be my child. You will live with me as my own."

"Karki!" Jhuma lifted her head and looked at him. Pearls were glittering in his eyes. Then she was overcome, and she covered her face.

"No, it cannot be. Why should you be pulled down into a ditch for my sake? You have such a big house and land, fields, property . . . how can it be? I will not add this sin to the other."

"What do these lands, fields, and property matter? I would not care even if my life were given away for you, Kanchi Didi! Only this heart of mine knows how much it is steeped in love for you. It was only because I had not won you over that I did not say anything before."

Then Jhuma looked up once again. She saw the tears streaming from his eyes. Today she saw real love. Love was not the joyful fun of youth. Real love made sacrifices and wanted nothing in return. The effect of love was felt in the heart. So even if the thing that was loved was far away, the heart still fostered its love, and this was something that never ended. The love that emerged when one was engrossed in physical attraction was not love: it was an adolescent delight, it was desire. It lasted for two days, then it died. This she understood clearly today.

Today Jhuma saw Karki as he really was. That Karki, whom she had not considered especially important, whom she thought of as a passing breeze that bore no thunder or rain: how great he was! How unworthy she was of him! She remembered the soldier and compared him to Karki. One was the moon in the heavens who gave the world coolness and showed the way in the dark. The other was a blazing flame in the burning wind of Chait who inflamed tender hearts and then became a heap of ash. An ocean was rippling in Karki's eyes, and Jhuma was wandering through a garden of imaginings. Her imagination found its way with its eyes, and it became a stream and mingled with the ocean. As she recalled how badly she had treated Karki in the past, Jhuma hung her head in shame, and after a long while she said, "But there's no question of living in this village, is there! We might leave, but where can we go? By the morning everyone will know that we are missing. As soon as we reach the border checkpoint we will be caught."[70]

Karki wiped his eyes. "Don't worry about that. I am a man who is always alone. My house is always locked up. No one will accuse me; no one will suspect that we two have gone off together. Yesterday someone paid off his debt to me, so my hands are not empty at present. We'll go now and get all the money I have, and this evening we will set out. We will be far away by the morning, and once we have crossed the border I will send a letter to your brother here. That will get them out of trouble; even the villagers will not be able to do anything to them once the thing has been settled."

"But where will we go, what will we do?"

"Once the Lord has shown us the way, something will turn up. From now on you need not worry at all. Your husband will be with you."

Jhuma took one look at Karki, and then she laid the whole load of her body at his feet. Karki lifted her up and hugged her to his breast. Then he pulled a box of sindur from his waistcoat pocket, wiped Jhuma's eyes, and rubbed the sindur into the parting of her hair.[71] With tears of joy, Jhuma again pressed her face against his chest. Then both of them set out for Karki's house to prepare to take their leave of the village forever.

◇ 28

A person may be happy, a person may be sad, but time goes on passing. Even if the lives of hundreds of thousands are going to end during the next half hour, the clock will not stop. The months of Asar and Saun: sometimes showers of rain, sometimes the burning sun; sometimes there is maize flour to eat, sometimes millet mash, sometimes just nettle leaves and water. Thus the days passed, and the time came near for Dhané to pay back the money he owed.

Moté Karki had written him a letter and told him everything, and so in a way he did not fear for Jhuma anymore. Nonetheless, from time to time he was mocked in the village, and many

pretended ostentatiously that they would not accept water in his house. But Dhané paid no attention to any of this and just went about his business, putting up with it.

The closer the date approached, the more anxious he became about the money. He asked many people for a loan and clasped his hands in front of the Sahus, but he met with no more success than a child who claps his hands to make a star fall from the sky. In the end he decided that he had no option but to give up his house and land.

Seven days before the deadline, the day when the Sahu would confiscate his land and throw all his belongings out of his house, Dhané went to Nandé. Nandé sat smoking on a bed on his verandah. He said, "What, have you come to pay the money today? There are still a few days left, you know!"

"Yes, I have come to pay you seven days early. Call the subba and the mukhiya and get them to reckon up the value of my land. You can take my land. If I am to get a few pennies myself, I will take them."

"What, are you planning to move out?"

"Not because I am happy to do so. You people have wiped out my place to live."

"No, we haven't wiped it out, you serf! I bought you oxen and gave you some fields, and I told you to make use of them. But you went mad and killed my buffalo, and now what's this you're saying? If you sell your property, you'll get a little for your travel costs. If you go into Madhes, you'll get some work to feed you![72] Or will you head for Mugalan?"

"I don't know where we'll go when we leave. Wherever the Lord takes us."

This was what Nandé wanted: that Dhané should move out so that he could acquire his property. He was in need of another property so that he could set up one of his nephews on it. He said, "If you want to sell your property, come tomorrow. I'll call them all here. Then tomorrow we'll make up the accounts, and you'll get whatever's outstanding. If you can't come, I'll register the transaction in your name at the office."

The next morning, all the big men of the village gathered in Nandé's yard to decide Dhané's fate. Dhané was sitting in a corner looking disconsolate. He was anxious about one thing: how much would they value his property at? Once the Sahu had been paid off, would there be a little left over for the journey, or would that disappear as well? He could not stop worrying about this. A price was decided on for the house and yard, all the contents of the house, and the livestock. Papers were drawn up and signed. When the Sahu's money had been subtracted, it turned out that Dhané would receive seventy-five rupees. But Nandé took pity on a person who was leaving all this forever, and he let him off two months' interest and put eighty-five rupees into Dhané's hand instead.

29 ◇

As Dhané walked up the path, the sun was touching the hills in the west. Tersé Lamichhane's house was on this path, and because Dhané owed him five rupees, he stopped. Tersé was sitting outside on his verandah. Dhané pulled five rupees from his waistband and gave it to him, saying, "Here! Daju, I borrowed this the other day. Also, I haven't paid you back for the meat we had last year. What to do? My house and land are lost. I'll be leaving tomorrow or the day after, I expect."

Tersé understood. "Do you have to take the whole family with you?" he asked.

"I'll have to take them, how can I leave them behind? So much for living in this place, it seems! And I doubt we'll ever meet again." Dhané wiped a tear from his eye.

Tersé's eyes moistened, too. He did not take the money from Dhané but said, "Feed those children on your journey. I don't need it. We are in the same position. How long does it take to lose everything, after all? If I could have helped you out with a few hundred rupees, today you wouldn't be leaving the place of your fathers. But what can be done?"

Although Dhané pressed him, Tersé would not take the money, so he put it back in his waistband and took his leave.

Dhané did not come home until the evening. Maina was standing in the yard looking out for him, but he went indoors and sat beside the hearth. Maina sat down next to him, and Dhané explained everything to her.

"Get everything packed right now," he said. "We must be off first thing in the morning. I have no wish to live in this sinful place anymore."

"We have to leave the place where we have lived for ages? This house is still damp with the sweat of your fathers! Must we leave right away?" Maina covered her face with her hands.

Dhané stroked her hair. "What can be done? What's the point of crying when fate has written this on our brow?" He consoled Maina, wiping away her tears with his hand. But who was there to wipe the tears that fell from his eyes onto her hair? Dhané was there to comfort Maina; as long as he remained, Maina did not have to take responsibility. But to whom could Dhané turn? There was only the Creator for him to place his hopes in. But at this time the Creator was sitting a little way off and mocking him.

◇ **30**

With the cock's first crow, three people come out of the main door. Dhané is in front, with some homespun cloth tied in a bundle on his back and some rugs bound around it. From his hand there hangs another small bundle. Behind him comes Maina, sobbing quietly, with their son on her back and a small bundle in one hand. Absentmindedly, Dhané wipes his eyes. The little boy is crying because his sleep has been interrupted.

The two of them came out into the yard and stared at the empty house. Maina's gaze fell upon the *tulsi* at the edge of the yard.[73] She set her bundle down on the wall, went back inside, and came out again carrying a small earthenware pot filled with water. As she poured water onto the tulsi, she muttered, "Soon you will probably wither and die. Who will come to give you water? And when will I ever be able to offer water to your tree again, Narayan?"

"Hey, that's enough! Let's go!" Dhané shouted.

Maina could hear her doves cooing in their nesting hole, and she went back inside once more. The child was howling with all his might, but she was not minded to comfort him. She felt around in the darkness inside, searching for another small earthenware pot. At last she located it and shook out a handful of grain. When she took the grain to the doves' nesting hole and offered it to them, they were startled.

"Who will feed you when we are gone? What will become of you? Who will fill his stomach with you?" She wept bitterly, leaning her head against the doves' ledge. Again, Dhané shouted to her from outside, "It's getting late! What is that woman doing?"

Suddenly Maina remembered the oxen, and she hurried to their stall. When they saw her the oxen blew through their nostrils: "phu, phu." Maina gave them some of the hay that lay nearby and stroked them. The words came mechanically from her mouth, "Today your new masters will come. They will give you tasty fodder and mash. . . . Don't ever kick anyone, work honestly, or else you'll be beaten. . . ." She was overcome by her feelings, and tears poured from her eyes.

After a while she calmed herself and went back to the yard. There she stepped into the granary and took a good look all around. Every object in there—the millstone and the husking machine, and even the beams, pillars, and roofpole—gave her plenty to remember and weep over for the rest of her life. To one side, an old nanny goat was tied up, and beside her a pair of kids lay chewing their cuds in the straw. As Maina came near, the goat bleated at her, and she stroked it. She picked up the small kids, set them on her lap, and put her cheek against theirs. It looked as if the three beings were whispering to one another. Outside, Dhané shouted with growing impatience, and Maina stood up, wiped her eyes, and came out. Dhané had already stepped out onto the main path, and she picked up her bundle and followed him.

The departure of these three people made a pitiable, utterly pitiable, sight. The departure of three people: husband, wife, and small son. Time and again they turn to look back, and then they go on. It is difficult to find something that compares with their journey precisely. If there had been an onlooker there at this time he would surely have been reminded of Lord Ram's exile in the forest. Ram went into exile in the forest for fourteen years, and then he came back. But these three have locked up their house and are leaving forever. Their hearts hold no hope at all of ever returning to this place.

Their journey will not lead them to reside in a forest or to reside in a house. Their journey is not planned. They are setting out without knowing where they are going. Where is this journey leading, where will it end, where is its destination? Probably even they do not know.

The house, shed, garden, and granary: all are still, as if the life has gone out of them. Dhané and Maina always used to greet the sun from the garden. Maina would rise to bathe very early, and then she would fetch a jug of water and wait in the garden to offer it to the sun. But today there would be no one there to offer the risen sun a stream of water from that garden.

With the first rays of the sun today, Dhané and Maina's new life will begin. Perhaps it will be better than their past, or maybe it will be worse. Whatever happens, one thing is certain: when the sun appears to them they will be far, far away from this house, garden, and yard where they spent a very large part of their lives. Far, very far away.

AFTERWORD: NEPALI CRITICS AND *BASAIN*

Basain is regarded by Nepali literary scholars as a work of social realism (*samajik yatharthavad*). Krishnachandra Singh Pradhan argues that the novel is primarily a portrayal of village society and that for this reason "the social circumstances of a person's outer life take the foreground, rather than his inner life. Although Dhané is the hero, the society described in the novel is its central reality, and the author is conscientious in his description of it" (1980:255). Pradhan goes on to say that Dhané's dispossession is the "economic aspect" (*arthik paksha*) of the novel, while the flight of Jhuma and Moté Karki is its "social aspect" (*samajik paksha*) (257). Although the baidar to whom Dhané forfeits his livestock and Nandé Dhakal to whom he forfeits his home are in a sense the authors and beneficiaries of Dhané's plight, Pradhan argues that they act strictly within their rights and are not really at fault: the fault lies in the way the society in which they live is ordered. This is the context within which all the characters make their choices: Dhané's are sometimes rash, and he has to face the inevitable consequences.

Rajendra Subedi describes *Basain* as "an example of idealized reality" (*adarshonmukh yatharthata*) (1996:91). He argues that, although it is an honest portrayal, it proposes no solutions for the problems it identifies:

> Unable to swim in a sea of debt, Dhan Bahadur goes abroad [*videshincha*]. The soldier makes Jhuma pregnant and satisfies his selfish ends and goes abroad, and Moté Karki takes Jhuma and goes abroad because he fears that his reputation will be tarnished by his acceptance of a wife who has been made unchaste by another man. Both kinds of disorder are the realities of the society of that time. But when Dhan Bahadur departs he leaves the oppression of a feudal and exploitive character like Nandé Dhakal unaltered, and when Moté Karki departs he leaves an immoral philanderer like the soldier to his own devices. Both Nandé Dhakal and the soldier are criminals, in both economic and moral terms, and they are spared the punishment for their crimes. (92)

Subedi's criticism of the novel is perhaps a mark of the Marxist influences that have entered Nepali literature and literary criticism in recent decades and given rise to a style of fiction termed socialist realism (*samajvadi yatharthavad*), which first appeared around 1950 and still retains some currency today. Socialist realism requires a more incisive class-based analysis of character and society, and although Dhané's reflections on his fate contain hints of an incipient political consciousness, this analysis is largely absent from *Basain*. Chettri writes that he had heard of Marx and Marxism when he wrote the book and had a nodding acquaintance with Marxist ideology, based on his reading of some pamphlets published by the Communist Party (of India, presumably). He believes that his understanding of Marxism might have contributed to the atmosphere of the final sections of the novel and admits that it made him "somewhat impassioned" (*kehi bhavuk*) as he was writing it (1992:36). That the villains of the piece are never confronted with their crimes may disappoint the seeker of fictional justice, but this is probably in closer accord with the reality the novel sets out to describe.

NOTES

FOREWORD

1. For instance, when they enumerate something, the characters of this novel use the old formula of *goda* (an old form of the numeral classifier *-vata* that follows the numeral in modern Nepali but precedes it in this style of language) + the number + the numeral *ck,* "one." Thus *godaduek* = 2, *godatisek* = 30, and so forth.

2. These terms are explained in more detail in the notes to my translation of the novel.

3. "Bitter-leaves" is a literal rendering of the plant's Nepali name, *titepati*. Shrestha (1979:36) and Turner (1930:283) both translate it as *"artemisia vulgaris."*

4. Bangdel's *Muluk Bahira* is discussed in Hutt 1998 and in more detail, along with discussions of Bangdel's other novels, in Chalmers 1999. Both articles contain excerpts in English translation.

1. Phagun: mid-February to mid-March.

2. *Baidar* is probably a corruption of the word *bahidar* and is defined by Turner as "clerk, writer" (1930:459). The baidars fulfilled an important role in village communities in eastern Nepal, acting as advisers to village headmen on legal issues and drafting documents for them.

3. A proverb meaning that livestock can never be a sound or permanent investment because of its vulnerability to disease, old age, natural calamities, and so on.

4. In the old currency system, an anna was one-sixteenth of a rupee.

5. Dhané is the diminutive form of Dhan Bahadur's name, and the name is chosen ironically: *dhan* means "wealth" and *dhané* means "wealthy one."

6. Cowrie shells were a common form of currency in rural areas of Nepal before the economy became centralized and monetized.

7. Nepali prose narratives such as this switch between present and past tenses more frequently than an English translation can reflect. The present tense is often used to depict physical settings or to analyze psychological or emotional conditions, producing a period of reflective stillness in the text, while the events of the story are usually recounted in the past tense. In this text, the present tense is also sometimes used to recount the unfolding of events, and this is reflected in the translation as far as possible. There are a few instances, however, where a paragraph begins to describe events in one tense and then switches to another for no apparent reason: the translation departs from the original in such instances so that this switching between tenses (which can be confusing in English prose) does not occur within the body of a single paragraph.

8. The baskets (*doko*) are carried on the back and shoulders and secured by a strap (*namlo*) around the forehead. The *ghum* is a boat-shaped covering made of interlaced bamboo strips that protects its carrier from the rain.

9. Kahila means "Fourth Eldest Son." Very few characters in this novel are addressed by their given names, and this reflects colloquial speech, in which kinship terms and birth-order names are used much more commonly. The birth-order names that occur in this novel are Kancha (m), Kanchi (f): "Youngest"; Kahila (m): "Fourth Eldest"; Sahinla (m): "Third Eldest"; and Jetha (m), Jethi (f): "Eldest." A *dhami* is a shaman or diviner.

10. *Bankalé*: a malevolent forest spirit.

11. The Damai are an artisanal caste who traditionally work as tailors. They occupy a low position in the caste hierarchy.

12. "*Jadau*" is a deferential greeting used by lower castes when addressing a member of a higher caste (Turner 1930:207). Leute's use of this form of greeting would appear to contradict the author's claim that he "did not need to defer to anyone": the inference is perhaps that the status acquired by birth remains a more powerful factor than any status acquired though wealth. Alternatively, in view of the ensuing tirade, it could also be construed as sarcasm.

13. Bulls are not generally confined but permitted to wander at will and are often held up as symbols of lustfulness and irresponsibility.

14. A *mohar* is half of one rupee.

15. Chait: mid-March to mid-April.

16. Bhadau: mid-August to mid-September.

17. Nani: "Child"; Bahini: "Younger Sister."

18. Limbugaon: literally, "Limbu Village."

19. A *kos* is a notoriously vague measure of distance that is usually

defined as two miles but sometimes as "the distance that can be covered on foot in half an hour."

20. Nepali has a complex pronominal system. The informal second-person pronoun, similar to the French *tu,* is *timi,* while the politer version, similar to the French *vous,* is *tapai.* The soldier uses the latter on this occasion.

21. Strictly, the term *dai* means "elder brother," but it is used more generally to address or refer to men who are older than the speaker, and here it clearly refers to the soldier's cousin.

22. Dhané's family name, Basnet, proclaims his Chetri (*kshatriya*) caste. He either knows that the soldier belongs to the same caste (nowhere in the story is his caste or ethnicity made explicit) or assumes that he does because of the soldier's occupation (in the classical *varna* hierarchy, the *kshatriya* are kings and warriors).

23. Bhaujyu: "Elder Brother's Sister."

24. The literal meaning of *sangini* is "female friend." Sangini songs are sung as dialogues between women, particularly among the Chetri caste (according to Weisethaunet 1997) and especially in eastern Nepal. The singers exchange their joys and sorrows in song.

25. Mugalan: an archaic and, it seems, exclusively Nepali name for India as the land of the Mughals.

26. The festival of Teej (*tij*) falls during late summer, on the third day of the bright half of the month of Bhadau (mid-August to mid-September). It is a women's festival celebrated almost exclusively by Bahuns and Chetris, during which a woman must undergo purificatory fasting to ensure the long life of her husband. Traditionally, women indulge in a feast on the eve of the festival, and on the day itself they dress in their red wedding saris and dance before temples dedicated to Shiva—activity that represents "a complete reversal of the Hindu ideal of womanly behaviour" (Bennett 1983:225). Teej is

followed by the festival of Rishi Panchami, on the fifth day of the bright half of Bhadau, during which Bahun and Chetri women purify themselves by taking ritual baths in a river. For further detail, see Bennett 1983:218–34.

The Sorah Shraddha is a collective honoring of all the ancestors of a lineage during the fortnight leading up to the festival of Dasain.

Dasain is the major social and religious event of the year, especially for Bahuns and Chetris. The warrior goddess Durga is worshipped during the Nine Nights (*navaratri*) leading up to the tenth day of the bright half of the month of Asoj (mid-September to mid-October), when the festival reaches its climax. Family members renew their kinship ties by daubing one another's foreheads with a mixture of yogurt, red powder, and rice in an action known as "giving *tika*." Animals (principally goats) are sacrificed and eaten during the festival, and the head of each household must provide each family member with a new set of clothes.

27. "Victory to the goddess Bhairavi!"

28. A song sung during the Dasain festival in honor of the great goddesses of Hinduism.

29. In his study of Chetri households, John Gray records that maize was generally considered to be the least desirable staple, far inferior to rice. His informants often described poorer or lower-caste households in terms of the fact that they had to eat *dhiro*, a maize flour paste, for their main meals, instead of rice or wheat (1995:133).

30. *Budho* is an adjective meaning "old"; "Budhe" is used as a nickname here, meaning "oldie." The Kami are an artisanal caste who traditionally work as blacksmiths. Like the other artisanal castes, they occupy a lowly position in the caste hierarchy.

31. A woman's *peva* is usually simply her dowry (more commonly called *daijo*). In some instances, it can denote possessions that a woman

brings to her husband's home when she marries him but that remain her own personal property.

32. Kubera, the king of the Yaksha and Kinnara demigods, is proverbially wealthy.

33. The *hat bazar*, a temporary open-air market that is set up regularly at a particular location on a particular day of the week or month, is an important feature of social and economic life in the hills of eastern Nepal (see Sagant 1996:213).

34. Kanchi Didi: literally, "Last-Born Elder Sister."

35. *Moro* (m) and *mori* (f), derived from the word for "corpse," are used as terms of either abuse or endearment, depending on the intentions of the speaker and the tone in which the word is uttered.

36. The traditional measures of weight or capacity are gradually being displaced by the metric system in Nepal today, but they retain their currency in many rural areas. A *pathi* is equal to 8 *mana*s, a *mana* being equivalent to 0.7 liters or about 20 ounces of grain.

37. *Khasi* goats are castrated goats, reared especially to be eaten.

38. *Khet* is fertile irrigated or irrigable land, usually located at some distance from a farmer's house, while *bari* is nonirrigated land. The general pattern is that during the wet season, rice is grown on *khet* land and maize on *bari* land; in the dry season, wheat may be grown on *khet* land and either wheat or mustard seed on *bari* land. *Khet* land is valued more highly, both because it is more fertile and because it yields rice. A vegetable plot located close to a farmer's house is also known as *bari*.

39. Kanchi: literally, "Last-Born Girl" or "Youngest Sister."

40. "The most typical and sometimes the biggest markets emerge at a neutral, uninhabited place, a mid point in the jungle between those living at the bottom of the valley and those at the summits" (Sagant 1996:214).

41. The soldier uses the Hindi-Urdu words *lekin*, "but," and *kuch*, "something," in this sentence.

42. The English word "recruit" appears in the original.

43. Married women wear vermillion powder (*sindur*) in the parting of their hair. The episode is probably intended to demonstrate that the soldier has forgotten an aspect of his own culture, thus emphasizing his status as an outsider. This is amplified in the exchanges that follow.

44. *Naraz* means "angry" and is commonly used in Hindi and Urdu. References to anger in Nepali most commonly make use of the verb *risaunu*, and the word *naraz* is known only by those who have had some exposure to Indian plains languages.

45. *Accha*: a Hindi-Urdu word meaning "good" or "okay."

46. Ferris wheels or rotary swings (*roteping*) are erected on the edge of many rural villages for the Dasain festival.

47. In Nepali, *maula-nishana*. A *maula* is a rock or a stone on which an animal is sacrificed. Before the ritual takes place the *maula* is worshipped and sanctified. A *nishana* is a religious flag or banner.

48. On "bitter leaves," see note 3 of the foreword.

49. Marriage is often defined as *kanyadan*, that is, a father's gift (*dan*) of his virgin daughter (*kanya*) to the groom's family, symbolized here by his tying her to her husband with a shawl, as in the marriage ceremony. The idea of courtship is antithetical to the ideals of *kanyadan*. See Bennett 1983:71–73.

50. *Dobaté* means "situated at the junction of two (*do*) roads (*bato*)" but can also mean "a shopkeeper at a corner; a pedlar who swindles passers-by" (Turner 1930:320). Sahinla is a birth-order name meaning "Third Son." It might be that the name Dobaté (literally, "two ways" or "two-wayed") is intended also to imply that this character is two-faced or hypocritical.

51. Magh: mid-January to mid-February; one of the coldest months.

52. It is usual for a man to refer to and address a friend's wife as "Elder Brother's Sister" (Bhaujyu) if he is in the habit of addressing that friend as "Elder Brother" (Dai), and in fact it is deemed quite inappropriate for a man to refer to or address a friend's wife by her given name. This is perhaps a logical corollary to the custom by which men between whom there is no family relationship very frequently address each other using kinship terms, especially Bhai, "Younger Brother," and Dai or Daju, "Elder Brother."

53. The term "Sahu" is applied to anyone to whom a substantial debt is owed, whether he be the owner of the fields a farmer rents or a moneylender who has extended credit to him.

54. Baisakh: mid-April to mid-May; the first month of the year.

55. "*Bhorla* creepers": "The creeper, Bauhinia Vahilii, the leaves of which are used for making *ghum*, or leaf-umbrellas" (Turner 1930:484). "*Chilaune* trees" could be translated as "itching trees."

56. Mangsir: mid-November to mid-December.

57. Jeth: mid-May to mid-June.

58. Sagant describes a farmer's routine at the time of year when the rice is first sown:

In the evening, when everyone has gone home and the mud has settled in the paddy fields, the owner takes his basket and, standing at the edge of the fields, broadcasts the rice. For the next five days he floods the field. At dawn he rushes down the hill and lets in the water, allowing it to flow until evening. The first day he oversees the two casual labourers he has hired to repair the levees along the fields that are to receive the rice seed. The next day he is alone. But he must stay to be sure someone else does not divert the water into his own paddy field. These are the first in a series of water disputes that will go on for two months. (Sagant 1996:256–57)

59. Gharti is the name of a class of people descended from slaves who were freed from bondage by the Rana prime minister, Chandra Shamsher (r. 1901–29) or otherwise emancipated. Until the abolition of slavery in Nepal in 1924, people became enslaved through sale, as the punishment for a crime, or through debt bondage. Höfer warns that the name Gharti is "not solely applied to ex-slaves and their offspring. Gharti seems to be, at the same time, a reservoir for people of 'notorious' origin" (1979:130). *Sané* means "small one" or "minor"; the author clearly means to assign a lowly status to this character.

60. Surya: the sun deity, who rides his chariot across the sky.

61. Thuli calls Maina *Bhaujyu*, "Elder Brother's Sister," while Maina addresses her as *Nani*, defined by Turner as "baby, small child; girl; term of affection for a young woman" (1930:340). Maina refers to Jhuma as *Kanchi*, "Last-Born Girl," while Thuli refers to her as *Kanchi Didi*, "Last-Born Elder Sister."

62. The exchange labor system is known as *parma*:

In the parma system each household sends several members (usually women) to whomever is planting (weeding, harvesting) on a given day. In return, that household gets an equal number of free laborers when its planting day comes. Members of poorer families with less land to cultivate often work for wages instead of labor exchange. The wage for a male laborer in 1975 was six rupees and two measures of flattened rice plus midday snacks and a few cigarettes each day. Women earned only three rupees and one and a half measures of flattened rice for a day's work. The amount one must work in the fields is a clear measure of one's status. (Bennett 1983:23–24; see also Gray 1995:174–79)

63. Turner defines *abi* or *abai* as an "exclamation of surprise or fear (used esp. by women)" (1930:36). *Aabui* is one of several variants of this.

64. *Ficus nemoralis*, a small tree whose branches contain a milky white juice (Shrestha 1979:38; Turner 1930:314), hence the Nepali name, which means "milky."

65. Asar: mid-June to mid-July, i.e., in four or five months.

66. *Arati:* a ceremony in which the deity in a temple is worshipped each evening by moving a tray of burning lamps in a circle around its image; the ceremony is usually performed to the accompaniment of various hymns in praise of the deity.

67. The word translated here as "friend" is *mitini.* Females become one another's *mitini* and males one another's *mit* in a ceremony that includes an exchange of gifts and creates a lifelong bond of fictive kinship that extends even to mourning obligations.

68. Among traditional upper-caste Nepali Hindus, a widow must wear white clothing for a year after the death of her husband, as must the chief male mourner of a family in which a death has taken place. Widows must never again wear red, "even as a tika mark or hair braid" (Bennett 1983:107). Thus white is a color that is closely associated with mourning and death, and this explains Jhuma's choice of attire at this juncture in the story.

69. The Legal Code (Muluki Ain), which was first promulgated in 1854, is greatly concerned with rules of commensality and with distinctions between castes and groups whose members are either "water ac-

ceptable" (*pani calnya*) or "water unacceptable" (*pani nacalnya*) and either "rice acceptable" (*bhat calnya*) or "rice unacceptable" (*bhat nacalnya*). Of course the question of who a person might safely accept food and water from is also determined by that person's caste and ethnic identity. A person who breaks the rules of commensality by sharing food or water with someone who is for them "rice unacceptable" or "water unacceptable" may be punished in various ways, including caste degradation and exclusion from commensal relations with fellow caste members. The 1955 edition of the Legal Code still recognized the caste hierarchy, but the version promulgated in 1963 contained no regulations concerning caste interrelations (Höfer 1979:203). This novel was first published in 1957–58, so it may be assumed that the villager's reference to the Legal Code is to the 1955 version. Here, it is suspected that Dhané's family may have been polluted, and his fellow villagers are arguing about what should be done about it. Höfer notes, "certain decisions are left to the relatives and fellow caste-members as, for instance, the question of whether somebody who has violated the rules of commensality is to be excluded from commensality or not" (197).

70. Jhuma assumes that Karki is planning to flee the country and fears that he will be regarded as an abductor.

71. The rite of putting on the vermillion powder (*sindur halne*) marks the climax of the part of the traditional Bahun-Chetri wedding ceremony that takes place in the bride's enclosure. The groom sprinkles a line of vermillion powder onto the bride's forehead and then makes a red line with it in the parting of her hair. "The red powder in the part of the bride's hair symbolizes the groom's sexual possession of her. It is said that only after the groom has placed the vermilion mark can the bride call him husband" (Bennett 1983:87).

72. *Madhes*, literally, "Middle Country," usually denotes the Tarai lowlands of Nepal or, by extension, the plains of North India.

73. All Bahun and Chetri houses have a *tulsi*, or sacred basil plant, in one corner of their courtyard. This plant is worshipped as a representation of Vishnu, here called Narayan.

Bennett, Lynn. 1983. *Dangerous Wives and Sacred Sisters: Social and Symbolic Roles of High-Caste Women in Nepal*. New York: Columbia University Press.

Caplan, Lionel. 1970. *Land and Social Change in East Nepal: A Study of Hindu-Tribal Relations*. London: Routledge and Kegan Paul.

Chalmers, Rhoderick. 1999. "Where We Belong: Some Observations on Culture and Society in the Novels of Lainsingh Bangdel." *Journal of Nepalese Studies* 2, no. 2: 20–38.

Chettri, Lil Bahadur. 1992 (2049 b.s.). "'Basain' dekhi 'Brahmaputraka Cheuchau' samma" [From *Basain* to *Brahmaputraka Cheuchau*]. *Samkalin Sahitya* 9:34–45.

——.1989. *Towards Unknown Horizon: English version of Nepali novel "Basain."* Trans. Mr. Larry Hartsell. Gangtok: Ankura Prakashan.

——. 1957–58/1989–90 (2014 b.s./2046 b.s.). *Basain*. Kathmandu: Madan Puraskar Pustakalaya. Reprint, Kathmandu: Sajha Prakashan.

English, Richard. 1983. *Gorkhali and Kiranti: Political Economy in the Eastern Hills of Nepal.* Ann Arbor: University Microfilms International.

Gray, John. 1995. *The Householder's World: Purity, Power and Dominance in a Nepali Village.* New Delhi: Oxford University Press.

Höfer, Andras. 1979. *The Caste Hierarchy and the State in Nepal: A Study of the Muluki Ain of* 1854. Innsbruck: Universitätsverlag Wagner.

Hutt, Michael. 1998. "Going to Mugalan: Nepali Literary Representations of Migration to India and Bhutan." *South Asia Research* 18, no. 2: 195–214.

——. 1991. *Himalayan Voices: An Introduction to Modern Nepali Literature.* Berkeley: University of California Press.

——. 1989. "A Hero or a Traitor? The Gurkha Soldier in Nepali Literature." *South Asia Research* 9, no. 1: 21–32. Reprinted in David Arnold and Peter Robb, eds., *Institutions and Ideologies: A SOAS South Asia Reader*, 91–103. London: Curzon, 1993.

Nepali Brihat Shabdakosh [Concise Nepali dictionary]. 1983–84 (2040 b.s.). Kathmandu: Rajakiya Prajña Pratishthan.

Pradhan, Krishnachandra Singh. 1980–81 (2037 b.s.). *Nepali Upanyas ra Upanyaskar* [Nepali novels and novelists]. Kathmandu: Sajha Prakashan.

Pradhan, Kumar. 1991. *The Gorkha Conquests.* New Delhi: Oxford University Press.

Regmi, Mahesh C. 1978. *Thatched Huts and Stucco Palaces: Peasants and Landlords in 19th-Century Nepal.* New Delhi: Vikas.

Sagant, Philippe. 1996. *The Dozing Shaman: The Limbus of Eastern Nepal.* Delhi: Oxford University Press.

Shrestha, Keshab. 1979. *A Field Guide to Nepali Names for Plants.* Kathmandu: Natural History Museum.

Subedi, Rajendra. 1996 (2053 b.s.). *Nepali Upanyas Parampara ra Pravritti* [The Nepali novel tradition and trends]. Varanasi: Bhumika Prakashan.

Turner, Ralph Lilley. 1930. *A Comparative and Etymological Dictionary of the Nepali Language*. Reprint, New Delhi: Allied Publishers, 1980.

Wiesethaunet, Hans. 1997. *The Real Folk Music of Nepal: "The Nepalese Blues."* CD and booklet. Oslo: Travelling Records.